Mulligan Magic

Mulligan Magic

Deb Stover

JOVE BOOKS, NEW YORK

MULLIGAN MAGIC

A Jove Book / published by arrangement with
the author

ISBN: 0-7394-3318-0

A JOVE BOOK®
Jove Books are published by The Berkley Publishing Group,
a division of Penguin Putnam Inc.,
375 Hudson Street, New York, New York 10014.
JOVE and the "J" design
are trademarks belonging to Penguin Putnam Inc.

PRINTED IN THE UNITED STATES OF AMERICA

*For Maudeen Wachsmith—tireless supporter
of romance fiction, talented reviewer and writer,
lover of all things Irish, and dear friend.*

Go muirní cnoic na hÉireann thú, Maudeen.

Thank you to Kemberlee Shortland of All Ireland Travel for her tireless research assistance, and to Peter Shortland for providing the photograph of Mulligan Cottage that inspired the cover art for this book. All that for the promise of a pint . . .

Special thanks to tireless critique partners: Von Jocks, Mo Webster, Mary Chase, Peg McCool, and Trudy Doolittle.

Prologue

County Clare, Ireland—1783

Sinéad climbed the massive boulders surrounding the castle, where her sweet Bronagh had died. Feet planted firmly on the highest rock, Sinéad's old body shuddered with rage and sorrow.

She tilted her head back to gaze upward at the tower of *Caisleán* Dubh. " 'Tis a place of evil," she whispered.

Bronagh had taken her own life after Aidan Mulligan rejected her love. Sinéad glowered at the proud, stalwart tower. She knew a thing or two herself about lost love. Squeezing her eyes shut, she pressed her fist against her own broken heart, remembering.

She'd once been young and in love. Oh, he'd been a handsome lad, and for one summer, she'd believed he would ask for her hand. She believed it so completely, she had lain with him—her virginity but a memory. But he never asked. Instead he had married himself to his church—his love of piety and traditions stronger than the love he'd professed for her.

And now—*now*—he dared to deny sweet Bronagh the comfort of being buried on hallowed ground. Sinéad straightened to scrub away her tears, allowing rage to flood through her mind to drive away the grief. The sun dipped lower, casting a long shadow from the tower toward the village. The shadow pointed like an arrow toward the church.

Toward Fergus—the man Sinéad had once loved.

She shook her tightly clenched fists in the air, and an angry gale whipped her long, black skirt about her legs. In her many decades upon this earth, she had never used her powers for evil—never done deliberate harm.

Until tonight.

She rested her hands on the rough stone of the castle wall. Power pulsed through her frail frame. This morning she'd written and memorized the words, needing them to be perfect. And potent. Summoning all the will of her ancestors and the universe, Sinéad cursed *Caisleán* Dubh.

"A darksome curse on them that walke these halls. May they finde only death and miserie. No joying be withstood within these walls—much daunted by sore sad despaire they be! Until that cruell, disdayned destinie, beguile them torne asunder with her power. Rejoin the accurst for all eternity with her so fierce bewronged within this tower. And ende this spelle, forever, in that blessed hour!"

Thunder rumbled and lightning flashed. Sinéad lifted her open hands to the heavens and rain exploded from the sky in a furious torrent, washing Bronagh's blood from the rocks that had stolen her sweet, young life mere days ago. "So mote it be," Sinéad shouted into the storm.

"Stop this madness!" Strong arms encircled Sinéad's waist and dragged her away from the castle wall.

Fergus. It didn't matter now. Her spell was cast. She didn't struggle against his physical strength. The storm drowned out most of his words, but she knew the feel of him. The scent of his wet skin, and even the texture of his wool cape.

She'd once loved him.

Fergus dragged her across the rutted road to his church, pushing open the heavy door without releasing her. Out of the tempest he released her, and they stood staring at each other, their breathing ragged and echoing off the high stone walls—a ghostly reminder of the love they'd once shared.

"What have ye done?" he asked. His voice trembled. "Sinéad, what have ye—"

She met his gaze. "Bronagh will live and love again."

Fergus crossed himself, eyes haunted. "Sinéad, that's blasphemy."

"Nay. Denying that child a proper burial is *blasphemy.*"

He looked up sharply, his eyes narrowing. "She took her own life. The laws of the church—"

"Are wrong."

"No." He drew a shaky breath and released it very slowly. "Yer ways are wrong."

"But they be me own, and from an older tradition than yours." Sinéad turned toward the door.

"Ye risk yer immortal soul," he whispered wretchedly.

Though she practiced what he considered a pagan craft, she was also Catholic. His words stung, and Sinéad slowly turned to face him. "I do not care how many lives I suffer for this, *if* indeed I do."

"Yer *eternal* life is what ye risk."

"No." She shook her head, remembering the day he had told her his decision to become a priest. "Ye destroyed that long ago."

"This is not about . . ." He reached toward her, but stopped partway, closing his fist around air. "It was not meant to be, just as Bronagh and—"

"Stop!" Sinéad pointed her finger again. "Stop," she repeated softly. "You took me virginity when 'twas offered, then left me for your church. Now at least leave me dignity in the end. 'Tis done. Let it be."

His face darkened. "Wait." He came toward her and gripped her wrist. "Ask yerself . . ."

She struggled against his hold, needing desperately to distance herself from this man of her heart. Now they were both old, their lives spent. "Ask meself what?" She held his gaze in the semidarkness. "What, Fergus?" She saw him wince at hearing his given name from her lips. She should hate him for not loving her enough.

"How much of this madness is—" he leaned closer, his warm breath fanning her face "—is because of me? Us?"

"Ye flatter yerself." But his words had hit their mark. " 'Tis for Bronagh."

"I baptized her, watched her grow into a beautiful lass. I mourn yer niece, too."

"Then allow the child to be buried on hallowed ground."

"I cannot." He dropped his hands to his sides, his expression filled with helplessness. "I cannot defy the laws of God."

"Not God. *Man.*" Her breath hitched. "So bloody blind."

"Ye will be damned, Sinéad," he said, his expression pleading. "Forgive the Mulligans. Aidan grieves, too. He only did his father's bidding. His duty. Come to confession. *Save* yerself."

"Do not speak to me of duty." She heard the desperation in his voice, but would not let it sway her. " 'Tis too late for me."

"No, 'tis too late for Bronagh."

"Not yet."

Something shiny dangled from his fingertips—the silver crucifix she had given him so many years ago—a pledge of her love and devotion. Her promise to love him always. And something more . . . If he had ever guessed that she placed a protection spell on it, he never would have accepted it. Her heart stuttered to see that he had kept her gift these many years.

Turning her back on him she threw herself back into the storm. The doors of the church slammed symbolically behind her. Rain pelted her head and shoulders; she welcomed its power, for she had cast her spell in anger.

Would her lack of focus spill other energies into the curse? She never should have thought about Fergus today. Her battle was for Bronagh—the child Sinéad had conceived in love and borne in secret.

But Fergus had turned his back on Sinéad and sworn himself to his church. Bronagh was dead now, and her own father would never know the truth.

One

Real men don't apply for rent-a-pig jobs.

Nick Desmond squirmed in the soft waiting-room chair. Whoever "Mrs. F" was, she'd been insistent about meeting him—had promised him top pay with important perks.

As her bodyguard . . .

Just thinking about it made him shudder. Well, he was here, but he hated being here. Hated what he'd become . . .

Since his third birthday, all he'd wanted was to be a cop—one of New York City's finest. It was in his blood, just like his old man and his old man's old man. He needed a frigging family tree to keep it straight.

John Desmond had been proud enough to burst the day Nick—his only child—had received his gold badge. Dad never finished college, and though he was a well-respected police officer, he would never be a detective. Nick couldn't remember ever wanting anything as much as that gold badge, or ever being as happy as he was that day. He'd worked hard for it. Earned it. Deserved it, dammit.

Sure, he wanted a wife and kids someday—a home. Dad would've made a terrific grandpa. Nick's breath hitched and he cleared his throat.

Fate had other ideas. His second day as a detective he

was added to a special task force assigned to put an end to the Fazzini drug empire. His third day as a detective he received an anonymous threat—either look the other way, or lose what was most important to him.

The fourth day, John Desmond was gunned down on the sidewalk outside their apartment building. . . .

Nick arrived while Dad was still alive. The old man's last words had been about family, and about how proud he was of his son.

The department called it a random, drive-by shooting, but Nick knew better. He'd been warned. He tried for six months to prove his father's death had been murder, but for every step forward he took, three new barriers appeared.

Someone in the department was on the take. Someone important. And that someone had planted Nick to give the task force some credibility—the new detective with a clean nose. Whoever was in charge didn't want to take Nick out the same way they'd eliminated John Desmond, because that would have raised suspicion of an inside job. So, instead, they'd framed Nick. Planted evidence that *he* was a cop on the take.

After that, the world Nick Desmond knew and the future he'd dreamed of were gone forever. Even now, the irony, the unfairness, brought bile to his throat.

Shit. He needed a drink. Seemed as if he *needed* a drink more often than he wanted one these days. And Nick didn't like needing anyone or anything. He'd been there, done that, and set fire to the damned T-shirt.

Acid churned in his stomach, and he forced his thoughts in another direction. *Get a job—get a life.* Even framed ex-cops had to eat. He'd spent every waking moment and most of his nightmares trying to pin Dad's murder on Fazzini. He'd lived and breathed revenge, revenge, revenge.

What did he have to show for that? Not a damned thing. But he wasn't about to quit now—or anytime. He just had to have an income, too.

After adjusting his attitude he worked on the strangling tie and gave his collar another tug, for all the good it would do. Who the hell had invented neckties anyway? *Probably a woman.*

"Damn." He swallowed the lump in his throat and let his head fall back against the wall with a soft thud.

A blonde—a direct descendant of the inventor of neckties, no doubt—emerged from the inner office. A distraction just when he needed one most.

She eyed him over the rim of her black-framed glasses. "Mr. Desmond, thank you for waiting. Mrs. F will see you now."

Nick gritted his teeth as he stood. *Time to face my shitty future.*

Nick straightened his tie again and tugged at the hem of his sport coat. "Ready as I'll ever be. Lead me to Her Majesty."

The blonde arched a brow and pursed her lips. She looked like she'd been sucking lemons down at Martinaro's Fruit Stand.

"A word of advice, Mr. Desmond." The blonde's voice took on an uppity, nasal quality.

"Yeah?"

"Treat Mrs. F with respect."

"I treat everybody with respect, unless they give me a reason not to." He flashed her a grin as she spun around and marched through the door ahead of him.

"Detective Desmond, I presume?" a soft voice with a faint Irish lilt greeted as he entered the inner office.

Nick sucked in a breath and held it, forcing himself to face the owner of the voice. He'd come this far, so he'd damned well follow through.

A diminutive woman sat in a huge leather chair behind a massive desk, the epitome of little old lady—matriarch and queen mother rolled into one. A cap of curly white hair crowned a face delicately marked by the passage of time, but he'd be willing to bet his first paycheck that she'd been a real babe a few decades ago.

The old lady peered at him with piercing blue eyes. "My, but you are a tall one. I believe you'll do quite nicely, Detective."

Confused, he held up an index finger, prepared to question the woman, but hesitated. After all, he'd come here for a job interview, and she'd practically hired him on sight. "I'm a little confused. And, in case you missed it, I'm not a detective anymore."

"Tall, strapping, ice-blue eyes, gleaming black hair." She gave a satisfied nod. "Hollywood would call you Black Irish."

Nick held himself rigid. He'd sunk low enough to even discuss this position. The least he could do was hear her out, even if she didn't make sense. "Yeah. So?"

The old woman's eyes narrowed and an intensity shot from them and right through Nick. "Blood will tell," she said.

Nick tilted his head at an angle, studying her. "Whose blood?"

The ghost of a smile parted the woman's lips, revealing papery fine wrinkles in her fair skin. "No one's, if you do your job right."

Nick had to laugh. Shaking his head, he said, "You want a bodyguard?" *It's just a job, Desmond. Just a job.* He held his hands out to his sides, palms up. "I'm your man."

"So you are." She folded her hands on her desk. "You're dismissed, Trish," she said to her assistant.

"Yes, ma'am."

A moment later, Nick was alone with the most unusual woman he'd ever encountered. She seemed downright royal, sitting across from him in that oversized chair. *A frigging throne.*

"Have a seat, Mr. Desmond," she said, indicating a chair much smaller than her own. "We'll discuss your duties."

Nick arched a brow as he lowered himself onto the soft

and, no doubt, insanely expensive leather. "I haven't heard a job *offer* yet," he said. "Ma'am."

Again the regal nod. "True. I reviewed your credentials and checked your references before contacting you. You're the man I want for the job." She drummed her meticulously manicured nails on the desk's surface for a few minutes, then added, "Your salary will be five thousand to start."

"Five thousand a month is sixty grand a year. As a *bodyguard?*" He held his breath, trying to act cool when he really wanted to pump the air with his fist and shout *yes!* Instead he sighed, realizing this fell into the too-good-to-be-true category. "What do I have to do for that much money? If you have something illegal in mind, you're talking to the wrong guy."

"I know that, too."

She smiled, and he realized she wasn't as frail as she appeared. Her brain was razor sharp. The old woman was manipulating him, and definitely up to something. Something big. The gut instinct he'd relied on while on the force kicked into full gear.

"You misunderstood me." Her expression was bland—deceptively so, no doubt. "Your position will be twenty-four and seven. Live in, if you wish. Therefore, I'm offering you five thousand per *week,* Mr. Desmond."

"Holy shit." He shot out of the chair. *To hell with cool.* "Lady, you must be high on some kinda drug."

"Not at all."

"That's . . . over a quarter-million bucks a year." He sank into the chair again, the sound of a cash register ringing in his ears.

"I'll make a note that you're adept at mathematics, and I *hope* I won't need your services for the full year," she said, smiling like the proverbial cat that had caught the pissant canary. "Will you accept the position, Mr. Desmond?"

Nick steepled his fingers beneath his chin, trying to remain calm and rational while visions of dollar signs danced through his mushy brain. He had to clear his name—keep his nose clean. "You're sure nothing illegal is involved?"

"Probably not."

He snorted. "What, exactly, does 'probably not' mean?"

The woman fell silent for a few moments, obviously contemplating her next words with great care. "Some facts must remain confidential. You might consider that unethical. I consider it sacred."

Nick chewed his lower lip and stroked his five o'clock stubble with his thumb and forefinger. The rasping sound in his head wasn't loud enough to drown out the sound of money. Lots of money. More importantly, he'd be paid for doing something similar to police work. All right, so that was a stretch, but this was as good as it could ever be again until he nailed the bastard who'd destroyed him.

And murdered Dad.

He drew a deep breath, forcing calm, cool logic to his mind. *It's* too *good.* He closed his eyes for a moment, then pinned Mrs. F with his cop-after-answers look. "Why?"

"Why what?" She lifted her chin a notch, her expression emotionless.

And that made him even more suspicious.

"Why me?" He drew a deep breath. "And what do you expect for five grand a week? I'm not exactly your typical boy toy."

Her cheeks pinkened and she stiffened. "I assure you, I am not after a . . . a *boy* toy." Her expression softened. "However, if I were, I think you would do quite nicely."

Heat flashed in Nick's cheeks. The old broad had made him blush. *Jeez.* He'd seen it all and done most of it. No one—especially not a little old lady—should be able to make Nick Desmond blush.

"Well . . ." He combed his fingers through his hair again, knowing she probably realized by now it was a nervous habit. "So what *do* you want for all that dough?"

"I believe we get what we pay for." She lifted one shoulder and an innocent smile curved her lips. "I want discretion, loyalty, and the best bodyguard money can buy. I believe that's you."

"Hmm." She could've hired him as a simple bodyguard for a lot less, and he had a hunch she knew it. It wasn't as if he'd kept his dismissal from the police force a secret. In fact, he'd mentioned it when her assistant first called him to arrange this meeting. *Honest to a fault.* "Someone threaten you?" he asked, holding her gaze as he watched for any sign that she could be lying. He found none. Yet.

"Not directly. Let's just say the threat is implied." Her expression hardened, but she still didn't look away.

"Again, why me?"

"Because I can meet your price."

"I'm not for sale."

"I have something you want."

"What?"

"A man of many words, I see." She pursed her lips and folded her hands on the desktop. "Do you want to know who I am, Mr. Desmond?"

He shrugged, feigning disinterest. *Damn straight I want to know who you are, Granny Warbucks.* "What's the *F* stand for?"

She hesitated. "A name that shall live in infamy, I'm afraid." Something resembling regret clouded her eyes. "My husband was . . ."

Nick stiffened, sensing some serious shit was coming down. "Who?" He kept his voice steady, though the sudden urge to shout and slide into bad-cop mode struggled for supremacy. "Who was your husband?"

"Angelo Fazzini."

Fingers of ice burst from a frozen lump in Nick's gut and spread outward. Surely he hadn't heard her correctly. "Float that one by me again," he said, his voice as steady as he could manage.

"You heard correctly." She pressed her lips into a thin line. "I'm not proud of who and what he was. I didn't learn the true extent of his villainy until after his death."

"Villainy?" Nick hissed through clenched teeth to stave

off the fury. The hatred. "Talk about your classic understatement."

She inclined her head for a few seconds, then finally met his gaze again. "Forty-two years ago, Angelo Fazzini swept me away from Ireland with romance and pretty words. He was powerful and worldly. I was young. Innocent. Foolish." She rolled her eyes. "Now I am none of those things."

"Yet you stayed married to him." Nick gnashed his teeth. "You must have known about his connections." *Say it, Desmond. Say it.* "*Mob* connections."

"I denied it to myself. And, Mother Mary help me, I loved him. At least, I loved the man I thought he was." Self-deprecation etched itself across her face, furrowing her brow. She drew a deep breath and squared her shoulders. "I looked the other way, because I was raised to believe marriage was forever. The church would never have seen it any other way."

"So what changed your mind?"

A haunted look came into her faded eyes. "When I discovered our son had followed his father into the . . . business. By then, it was too late to prevent the inevitable."

Nick snorted again. Fazzini junior's New York drug operation was one of the most profitable and deadly in the whole damned country. The real culprit who had murdered Dad and destroyed Nick's career had gone free. Angelo Fazzini junior. Free.

The Fazzini operation had friends in high and low places. Cops on the take, politicians in their beds, and their thumbs on the national media. One dead officer and a destroyed junior detective didn't amount to shit compared to the big picture.

And now . . . he pinned his gaze on Junior's mother. The irony of it tasted bitter. He leaned forward, bracing his hands on his knees, elbows locked, every muscle in his body ready for action.

He tried to think of one good reason why he should accept the offer. *Besides the money.*

Bad money. Drug money. Blood money. The guilt would gnaw at him, and his ancestors would rise from their graves and hunt down any Desmond on the take.

Of course, Nick wasn't a cop now. Might never be again . . .

"I need a bodyguard who's as desperate as me. Someone I can trust," the woman said, her voice revealing some of the tension she'd managed to hide earlier. "For myself . . . and my granddaughter."

"You think I care what happens to Junior's kid?" Nick barked a derisive laugh and pushed to his feet. He had to get the hell out of here before he told the old lady *all* the horrors her husband and son had caused.

"Yes, I think you care," the woman said on a sigh. "Like I was four decades ago, my granddaughter is an innocent. My daughter-in-law found *her* escape from reality in the bottom of a bourbon bottle until she died." Mrs. F stared into the distance, then swung her gaze back to Nick and stood. "Help me save my granddaughter from her grandfather's evil legacy, Mr. Desmond. It's too late for me. My life is all but over, but I'll do anything I can to protect Erin. *Anything.*"

The woman's words reverberated through his head. There was something wrong with her story—something he should remember. "Wait . . ." He rubbed his temples and stared at her. "How many kids does Junior have?"

"Only one." The old woman shifted her gaze just enough to alert Nick that she was hiding something.

"What are you up to, lady?" he asked as he remembered the case in question. "Angelo Fazzini's only grandchild was kidnapped and never found. I was fresh out of the police academy when it happened."

The woman lifted her chin a notch. "That is correct."

"Well, gosh," he said, his voice dripping sarcasm, "color me confused."

"Erin wasn't kidnapped. Exactly."

"Holy . . ." Realization made him cough, but he couldn't

prevent the seeds of admiration germinating in his brain.
This woman had grit. "You?"

"Indeed."

"Why?"

She drew a deep breath and released it very slowly. "I
asked my son to give up his life of crime for his child. He
refused."

"Let me get this straight." Nick held up one finger.
"You kidnapped your own granddaughter and have kept
her hidden all these years?"

"Correct." No sign of remorse crossed the woman's
face. "I will do whatever is necessary to protect her,
though I failed her mother."

"What do you mean?"

She lifted her chin and her eyes blazed. "I have proof
that my daughter-in-law did not commit suicide. She was
helped. That knowledge was the catalyst that made me . . .
move Erin."

Nick released a low whistle. "You're talking about your
own flesh and blood here."

Her lower lip trembled a little, and she bit it. After a
moment she drew a deep breath. "My own son. My baby.
Now a monster. A killer of innocents."

Nick didn't have to tell her about the extent of Junior's
crimes after all. Even more importantly, he *believed* her. A
mother wouldn't turn on her own kid without damned
good reasons. She had those in spades. "Where is your
granddaughter now?"

"We haven't reached an agreement yet, Mr. Desmond."

"You're slick, lady."

"Thank you."

Nick grinned. "What's your plan?" he asked, wondering why the hell he was still here, yet knowing he would
not—could not—leave now.

"My granddaughter has spent these past years abroad,
in a private boarding school." She lifted her chin a notch,
her expression unwavering. "Now, at eleven, Erin wants

to leave there. She wants to live with me—her only living relative. So she believes . . ."

"But you can't bring her home."

"So you see my dilemma." Mrs. F lifted a shoulder. "My granddaughter is far too high-spirited for her own good sometimes."

High-spirited sounded like trouble to Nick. "Does she know who she is? More importantly, who her *father* is?"

"She doesn't remember, thank the Blessed Virgin," the old woman explained, shaking her head. "I placed Erin in an abbey school with a generous monthly allowance for the Sisters. The only name they, or she, know is my maiden one. I've visited often over the years, and taken her to the Continent for holidays, so Erin knows me well. As I mentioned, she and the Sisters believe I am her only living relative."

"Clever." Nick nodded his approval.

"Necessary."

"Now what?"

Angelo Fazzini's widow set her jaw and her blue eyes flashed with determination. "I've promised to take her to my home, though not here, of course."

"Keeping her hidden from your son's tentacles won't be easy."

"Angelo believes his daughter is dead." The woman's expression was solemn. "Besides, they won't think to look where we're going."

"And where *is* that?"

She narrowed her eyes again. "You haven't accepted the position yet, Mr. Desmond," she repeated. "How can I trust you not to reveal our destination until you've made a commitment?"

"Besides the money, give me one good reason to accept this crazy job."

A victorious smile spread across the woman's face. "A reason no red-blooded Irishman can refuse, Mr. Desmond."

"Try me, lady." He folded his arms across his abdomen and waited.

"Revenge."

Nick's heart skipped a beat and his breath lodged in his throat. "So that's why you chose me."

"Precisely." The old woman's smile had vanished. "I have the evidence you need. All of it. I can prove who murdered your father, and also who framed you."

He clenched his fists, his head pounding. "All right," he said. "I'll play. Give me the evidence."

She arched both brows, her expression one of open disbelief. "Once I'm certain that Erin and I are safe, you'll have the key to a safe-deposit box."

He wanted the evidence *now,* but he could tell this woman wasn't about to give it to him yet. Nick forced himself to concentrate on her words, though his lust for vengeance raged through his veins like a fever. "When?"

"A year at the most. Surely we'll be safe by then."

"A year?" He gritted his teeth. It sounded like forever, but he'd waited this long, and he could wait a little longer. He would have his revenge. Finally. "Not one day more than a year. Where are we going?"

"In a moment. You're a man of your word. Please remember that. A child's life—and mine—could be at stake."

Junior's mother was toast if her son ever learned what she'd done. The old lady had guts. "You have my word, and that's that. Where?"

"To the village your grandfather's family is from," she said. "Ballybronagh in the southernmost tip of County Clare."

"Ireland?" It might as well be another planet. He resigned himself. He'd be counting the days. "Good hiding place."

"I think so. My people were from County Cork, so no one there should recognize my maiden name." She pressed her lips into a thin line, her gaze never wavering. "You're a man in search of his roots, and your connection to Ballybronagh will help establish us there. Once that's accomplished, you will have your evidence and may do with it as you please."

He held up one finger, struggling against the urge to get soft. The lady had grit. "Not one frigging day more than a year."

"Agreed, Mr. Desmond." She narrowed her eyes. "And though I abhor violence, let me assure you of this."

"Yeah?"

"If you betray our location to *anyone,* even after that year . . . I will kill you myself."

Maggie Mulligan trudged along the familiar road between Ballybronagh and *Caisleán* Dubh. With a sigh she tilted her head back to gaze up at the dark tower, thrusting toward the sky. Gulls circled it, calling a cheerful greeting to the world below.

Once upon a time, *Caisleán* Dubh had been the most frightening of places. Well, now, *that* had certainly changed since Bridget's arrival in their lives. Riley and Bridget's marriage had broken the curse at last.

So why did Maggie feel so odd—as if she were being watched? *Now isn't that a bit of nonsense?*

After going back to university following her last visit home, her roommate, Ailish, had asked what had frightened her. Maggie had been unable to deny it, nor could she name any specific event. All she knew was that the uneasiness had started upon awakening on her birthday. She'd gone home to celebrate the day with her family, and had struggled with panic attacks every time she crossed the threshold of *Caisleán* Dubh. And the strange bouts of terror continued even now that she was home to stay.

Ailish, a Wiccan, had given Maggie a book about cleansing and protection rituals. Reluctant at first, Maggie hadn't yet opened the book. However, since coming home and encountering even more queer feelings, she'd decided it was worth a try. This was her home and she wanted to stay.

Unafraid.

Shaking herself, she considered how different her family was now. Riley was married to Bridget, young Jacob—her dear departed brother Culley's son—was now eleven, and Mum had moved from her precious cottage and into the once-cursed castle. Everyone's lives had changed.

Except Maggie's.

After graduation she'd returned to Ballybronagh, hoping to teach here. Instead she'd been told the school was closing due to lack of funds, and there were no openings for teachers in nearby Kilmurray.

She looked at the castle again. There would always be a job there for her, but it wasn't the same as making her own way. Her brother and sister-in-law had turned the old castle into a first-rate restaurant called Mulligan Stew. The renovations for the bed and breakfast were nearly complete. By autumn *Caisleán* Dubh would be open to overnight guests.

She paused, gazing out at the sea. She'd missed her family. Now she was home and she wanted to stay, yet she needed to work, too. She was incomplete.

"Well, if it isn't the graduate, herself."

Maggie jerked, surprised to see her brother scrambling over the stone wall behind *Caisleán* Dubh. She gave Riley an impatient glower, though inwardly she smiled. Since marrying Bridget almost four years ago, he seemed younger and happier than he'd ever been.

"'Tis trying to scare me half to death, you are, Riley Mulligan." She shaded her eyes against the afternoon sun.

"Not since you stopped trying to kill me with your vile cooking." He gave an exaggerated shudder.

"I'll not let you rattle me today, boyo."

"Ah, not even a bit of sibling rivalry for old times?" He jumped down from the wall and stood in front of her, tall and handsome as always. Angling his head slightly to one side, he narrowed his eyes. "Something troubles you."

She flashed him a halfhearted smile. "And couldn't you always read me?"

"That's well and good, so don't you be forgetting it."

She rose on tiptoes and kissed his cheek. "You'll always be my hero."

"What is it, Maggie?" he asked, his voice gentle. "What troubles you, lass?"

"I want to teach. I *need* to teach." She fisted her hands. "'Tis my dream, Riley."

"Ah." He pulled her into a hug, then set her away to stare into her eyes. "And teach you shall."

"There are no positions in Kilmurray or at the National School in Doolin." Her shoulders fell and she willed herself not to cry. She had her reputation to consider. "Jacob and the younger children will have so far to go to school."

"If we send him there."

"Riley Francis Mulligan, what nonsense is this?" Maggie jabbed him in the upper arm with her index finger. "Jacob is a bright boy—our own brother's son—and he needs—"

"Settle down, now." Riley rubbed her shoulders, his Mulligan blue eyes dancing. "He'll have his education, but we're thinking his Aunt Maggie should be his teacher."

She shook her head. "They don't have any openings in Kilmurray."

"I know, but . . ." He bit his lower lip and linked his arm through hers. "Walk with me, lass."

They headed beyond the castle wall and down the steep trail that led to the beach. As they passed the largest boulders near the tower, an icy chill filled her. She shivered and almost stumbled, but forced herself to keep up with Riley. Something was on her brother's mind. As they drew away from the tower, the chill passed, and she pushed her unfounded fear to the back of her mind.

"We kept this from you for a few months, since Bridget had that miscarriage two years ago." He drew a deep breath. "But now the doctor says 'tis safe to tell the whole world that she's expectin'."

"That's wonderful." She hugged him, but pulled back when she noted the tightness of his shoulders. "What is it, Riley? Is she all right?"

"The doctor says she's fine, but . . ."

"But what?" She held her breath, waiting. Bridget's miscarriage had been hard on the whole family, and worse for Riley. "If the doctor says she's fine, then—"

"She works so bloody hard." He released a long, slow breath. "From dawn till dark, she's in the kitchen of her precious Mulligan Stew, planning the day's menus, starting the sauces and such. Don't get me wrong. I love the work as much as she does, but . . . I worry." He lifted a shoulder.

"What does Mum say about it?"

A lopsided grin spread across his handsome face. "That I'm bein' a typical male."

Maggie had to laugh. "Well, then," she said. "There you have it."

"You know 'tis true." His voice softened. "Bridget works too hard. I want her to slow down, but she's driven."

"Driven by love." Maggie rubbed her brother's arm, savoring the sound of the ocean behind them. She'd missed Ballybronagh and her family so much. "I'll help, and so will Mum. We all will."

He grinned and his eyes twinkled. "Can you believe I'm to become a da?"

"Aye, Riley, I can believe it." She hugged her brother. "Haven't I watched the way you've been more than an uncle to Jacob?"

"You always know the right thing to say." Riley pulled her into a hug. "'Tis glad I am to have you home, little sister."

And home is where I'll stay. She gazed past Riley at the endless sea, determination filling her. Somehow, she would make it work.

They chatted as they climbed back up the cliffs to
Caisleán Dubh. Mum stepped through the side entrance
of the castle as they passed. She shook a rug until it surrendered its dust in desperation.

"Mum, you should save that for me," Riley said, taking
the rug from her. "How's Bridget?"

Mum chuckled. "The same as she was an hour ago."
Her gaze fell on Maggie. "Ah, 'tis good to see both me
children together again."

Maggie's eyes burned again as she released Riley's
hand and hugged her mother. " 'Tis good to be home,
too."

"Did you talk to her, Riley?" Mum asked, her hand still
resting on Maggie's forearm.

"About what?"

"I started to, but we got to talking about something
else."

"The babe, no doubt." Mum's eyes twinkled.

"And Bridget," Maggie amended. She rolled her eyes
and winked. "You'd think the lad was smitten."

"Isn't he, now?"

"All right, enough of that." Riley grinned, ruining his
attempt at sounding gruff.

The door behind Mum opened and Bridget stepped out,
her hand pressed to her still-slim abdomen, her dark hair
pulled back from her pale face. Riley moved to her side
quickly. "Are you all right, love?"

Bridget drew a shaky breath. "Still have a little morning sickness, but it's better than last month."

" 'Tis afternoon," Riley argued.

Bridget grimaced. "Tell that to my—" She covered her
hand with her mouth and darted back inside.

"Riley, it can happen anytime of day or night," Fiona
Mulligan said, patting her son's arm. "She's almost beyond that stage now. Don't worry so. Bridget's a healthy
lass, and she'll bear a healthy babe. Mark me words."

The worry remained in his eyes. "I wish I could do it
for her."

That made Mum and Maggie both burst into laughter. Riley blushed again. "Back to business," he said.

"You were supposed to ask me something." Maggie folded her arms across her waist, waiting.

"Help us keep the school from closing," he said. "I think we can raise enough, for at least this year."

"Teach?" Maggie's breath caught. "Here?"

"Aye." He looked toward the doorway again. "I'm going to check on Bridget. You give it some thought. We *can* raise enough money to keep our school, though your wages might not be much the first year."

Maggie blinked as her brother disappeared through the dark doorway in search of his wife. "Teach in Ballybronagh?"

Mum gave her hand a squeeze. "Brady Rearden thinks 'tis a grand idea, and so do I."

"Oh, aye, if we can make it work." She shook her head, still confused. "I'm not in any position to say no. I need to teach. 'Tis my dream."

"And the children need a teacher," Mum said in her practical way.

Excitement bubbled through Maggie. "All my life, I've wanted to teach right here in Ballybronagh. I thought all hope of that was gone."

"I know, lass." Mum brushed a stray curl away from Maggie's face. "And maybe one of these days you'll find a nice young man and get married."

Maggie rolled her eyes. Hadn't she heard this one before? "I'm not ready."

"So you say." Mum patted Maggie's shoulder. "All right, lass. I'll not speak of it again now."

But she would later. Fiona Mulligan wasn't one to give up easily. Didn't Maggie know that better than anyone? "Thank you."

"Well, let's start plannin' the fund-raisin'."

Maggie watched Mum's broad smile spread across her round face before the older woman went back inside the castle.

Maggie needed a moment to pull this new hope around her like a warm shawl. When she'd first heard of the school's closing, she feared she might have to leave Clare to find work. Now she had hope. Joyous hope.

She gazed toward the village, where the parish school sat next to the church. The children's playground butted up against the cemetery. The lot of it sat on a high knoll overlooking the sea. Wasn't it a grand spot?

Her gaze fell to the church, where she'd attended mass since birth. The stone building had stood for over a century. Beyond it, at the far end of the cemetery behind the school, sat the original church, now in ruins.

An odd sensation—almost like an extra pulse—reverberated through her. She lifted her hand toward the old church, took a step . . .

The side door opened again, and young Jacob bounded out, jarring Maggie from the powerful urge to visit the ruins and explore the school grounds right this minute.

"Jacob, you get taller every time I see you." The lad stood nearly as tall as Mum already. "Look at you. I've been home two months and you've grown every day."

"Are you really gonna be my teacher?" he asked, hugging her.

She laughed and ruffled his dark curls. "If we can raise enough money to keep the school open."

"We will." Jacob's enthusiasm warmed her. "Mamó says we'll have a *céilí* right here to raise money."

"That's a perfect idea."

"And Uncle Riley said he'll have enough Guinness and Harp to loosen even the tightest purses." Jacob grinned. "Whatever that means."

Maggie laughed. "Let's go wash up for supper now."

"And talk about the *céilí.*"

"I'll be right along." As Jacob disappeared through the doorway, she glanced back again to the village and the ruins. Twilight cloaked the village in shadows now, but the church and school remained bathed in watery sunlight. Even now, they seemed to be waiting for her.

Something glittered from the ruins. She blinked. When she looked again, the glitter was gone. She'd seen it before, but somehow it seemed brighter now.

"Enough silliness, Mary Margaret." She glanced back at the ruins again before entering the castle.

Aye, tomorrow she would explore her future.

Two

Nick glanced at his watch for the umpteenth time while waiting for his new employer. Kennedy was packed, as usual, and he was just a face in the crowd. As instructed. The anticipation ate at him.

The old woman had told him to dress casually in jeans and a T-shirt. She'd had no way of knowing, of course, that this was his standard attire. He looked across the terminal at the throng of people.

As promised, his first week's pay had been deposited directly into his bank account. At least he'd been able to confirm that before leaving the country. Weekly payments would be made until his tenure ended—at least, that's how she'd put it. He'd given up his apartment and put his meager belongings in storage.

Including his gun. How the hell was he supposed to play bodyguard against *serious* criminals without a gun? After Mrs. F had informed him that handguns were completely illegal in Ireland, he'd been researching various ways of obtaining permission to carry his weapon. No go. As a civilian, he didn't stand a prayer.

Bodyguard without a gun . . .

"Here's my nephew now," a robust voice said with an

overblown Brooklyn accent. "He'll help me find my gate. Thank you for your time, young lady."

Nick arched a brow. The woman with the accent climbed down from the little cart with the attendant's help. She had iron-gray hair in a wild, curly style—a cheap wig, he realized. Her clothes looked like something from the nearest thrift store—polyester pants, a wild floral shirt, and a purse just a shade smaller than New Jersey.

He grinned. She reminded him of Grandma.

She patted his arm and waved the attendant away. He was about to tell her she had him confused with someone else until she peered into his eyes from behind a pair of rhinestone-studded glasses.

"Holy sh—"

"Watch your language, Nicholas."

"Sheesh."

With a cunning smile she patted his arm again. "Come along now, or we'll miss our flight. Don't you worry. I have everything we need right here." She pointed to her giant purse.

Smiling again, she looped her arm through his and they headed down the concourse. "So, how do I look?" she whispered in her normal Irish-flavored voice.

He flashed her a grin. "Like hell. Even your own momma wouldn't recognize you."

"Groovy, dude." She looked down the corridor. "We need gate twelve in this section."

Once they reached their destination and the old lady had her granddaughter safely hidden, Nick would determine how the revenge she'd promised him would come into play. Right now, he had a job to do, and he intended to do it well. The old woman was rightfully worried about the consequences of Junior finding her.

As much as he would welcome the opportunity to come face to face with Fazzini and really earn his pay, he didn't want to put his employer and her granddaughter at risk. Hell, yes, he would enjoy defending them and offing Fazzini, but that wasn't enough. Even more than he wanted Fazzini dead, Nick wanted his own name cleared. At any rate, he now understood why his employer had been willing to offer him such a huge salary.

Right now, all he wanted was to do a good job . . . and to give Junior Fazzini exactly what he deserved. Maybe after he'd put Dad's murderer behind bars, he'd rejoin the force. Maybe . . .

Passengers were already boarding when they arrived, and Mrs. F maneuvered him into the line when the call went out for passengers needing extra assistance. She was one slick operator, which reinforced his earlier conclusion that the old broad bore watching. After all, she was Angelo Fazzini's widow. Even worse, Junior's mom.

He ignored the acid tornado in his gut as he handed his boarding pass to a uniformed woman who flashed him a thousand-watt smile. With a wink she returned the stub the machine spit back. Then they headed down the passageway and onto the plane.

"Welcome." Another attractive woman pointed him toward his seat in First Class. Well, at least that was something.

Mrs. F took the seat next to his, sliding her mutant purse under the one in front of her. She fastened her seat belt and pointed at his. "Buckle up." Her smile taunted him, and she shoved her gaudy glasses higher up on her small nose.

He looked down at his boarding pass. MR. N. DESMOND. He'd bet his first month's salary that hers didn't say Mrs. A. Fazzini. "What's your name anyway?"

Her expression grew wistful. "Maureen."

"Your real name?"

She nodded. "But from this day forth, my last name is O'Shea, and don't you be forgettin' it, lad."

Lad, my ass. He looked out the window, then back at her, lifting one corner of his mouth. "I thought I was your long-lost nephew."

"Aunts don't always have the same last name, boyo. Be

glad you're not my son, or you'd have to call me Mum."
She leaned her head back against the plush, leather seat.

"Mum?" Nick shook his head. "Not in this lifetime."

"You may call me Aunt Maureen. Will that be easier on
your macho sensibilities?"

He shook his head, waggling his eyebrows at her.
"Aunt Mo."

She heaved an exasperated sigh. "You're annoying your
sweet, old auntie."

Nick grinned. "I know."

"Erin calls me *Mamó,* so Aunt Mo sort of . . . goes with
it, I suppose. Call me anything except that F name. She's
dead now. Gone."

He studied the old woman for a few minutes. "Won't
your son look for you?"

She stiffened, pressing her lips into a thin line. "He will
search for my body, I suppose."

"Say what?" Nick narrowed his eyes, waiting for the
woman to explain.

She looked around, then leaned very close to him.
"This evening, my private plane will take off for Nan-
tucket."

"I don't follow."

"There will be no passengers, and the pilot will para-
chute to safety before the plane crashes into the Atlantic.
He's been well paid for his discretion."

"I'm assuming there will be a boat waiting for him, too.
Right?"

"Of course. All the arrangements have been made."

Nick made another mental note to keep a close eye on
his employer. "You're even more devious than I thought."
He was really starting to admire this old woman, regard-
less of her name.

She lifted a shoulder. "The only way to begin a new life
with my granddaughter is to end my old one."

He had to admit that she made a lot of sense in a sick
sort of way. "So . . . the pilot bails and the plane crashes—
there are no survivors?"

"Precisely." She gave him a weak smile. "Now will you let me take a nap?"

"One more observation first?"

"If you must."

"I must." Nick chewed his lower lip and asked, "How can you have a nephew, since the kid thinks you're her only living relative?"

"Ah." Aunt Mo seemed taken aback. "A minor detail I overlooked."

"Well, you're paying me, so I figure I oughta help make sure you don't overlook any more minor details." Nick grinned.

"You're my long-lost nephew—one I didn't know about." She arched a white eyebrow. "I'll figure out the missing branches of my family tree later. *Now* can we get some rest? Planning my own demise and rebirth has been exhausting."

"Good morning, ladies and gentlemen," a woman said over the speaker. "Please give your attention to the safety instructions . . ." The woman stood in the aisle, pointing to all the exits, and explaining how the seats could be used as flotation devices.

"Flotation, my ass." Nick glanced dubiously at the seat beneath him. He could handle flying, but bobbing around in the ocean didn't set well with him at all. Not after seeing *Titanic* and *Jaws*, thank you very much.

A few moments later the jumbo jet rumbled down the runway and rose gracefully into the sky. He watched in silence until the shoreline had almost vanished. Fluffy white clouds eventually obscured his view.

The attendant started speaking over the intercom. "Welcome to Flight eighteen oh one, with nonstop service to Shannon Airport."

"I guess it oughta be easy enough to disappear there," he whispered.

"Have you ever been to Ireland?"

"I've never been anywhere." *Except to hell and back a couple of times.*

Since the day Fazzini's thug had murdered Dad and shattered all of Nick's dreams, he hadn't allowed himself to think—consciously, anyway—about his future beyond revenge. No, he never allowed his thoughts to go farther than one day at a time. Dreams didn't count. Real life wasn't like that. Why waste time thinking about what might have been?

And what could never be.

Erin O'Shea waited in the dim hallway, secreted behind the Reverend Mother's office door. She'd waited long enough for Mamó. Her grandmother had promised to come for her, and Erin couldn't stand the waiting one more minute. Somewhere in Reverend Mother's office, there had to be a file with a phone number.

She'd never been allowed to call her *mamó* by herself. Reverend Mother had always retrieved a file and dialed the number for Erin. After asking for Maureen, she would pass the phone to Erin.

Well, this time Erin O'Shea would call Mamó herself! She was eleven, and certainly old enough to call her own grandmother.

Finally, Reverend Mother glided out of her office with her long black skirt sweeping the floor and her veil hanging down her slim, straight back. Though Reverend Mother had never been unkind to Erin, she was a bit stern at times.

Even so, Erin refused to feel guilty as she stole into the office and opened the file cabinet. She leafed through and found one with her name. Her fingers trembled a bit as she pulled out the form containing the required information.

The phone number was written in red, and beside it the words EMERGENCY ONLY were stamped. Erin hesitated. But this was an emergency. Mamó had promised her a normal life, a real home, and she'd said she would arrive before Erin's birthday.

Today.

Erin dialed the number and waited for a series of clicks. After four rings she heard her grandmother's voice—a recording. She waited until the tone, then said, "Mamó, it's Erin. When are you coming for—"

Footsteps sounded in the hallway. Erin hung up the phone and shoved the paper back into the folder, silently closing the file drawer. She darted around the desk and stood with her hands clasped before her. Innocently, she hoped.

"Ah, Erin, there you are," Reverend Mother said as she glided into her office. "I was about to send for you."

"You were?"

The slender woman smiled. "Your grandmother is on her way from the airport now."

Relief and guilt washed through Erin, but joy overshadowed both. She clapped her hands together. "Thank you. Oh, *thank* you." She threw her arms around the woman who had raised her. "I'll miss you."

Reverend Mother sighed and stroked Erin's hair. "And I you, lass."

"I'll visit you."

"I'd like that."

Erin remembered the phone call she'd made, and wished she hadn't done it. Guilt gnawed at her.

"Go to your room and pack your things now." Reverend Mother hugged Erin again. "You don't want to keep your grandmother waiting."

"I'm going home." A sense of wonder spurred Erin down the hall to her room, phone calls and waiting all but forgotten.

At the now vacant Mulligan Cottage, in the shadow of *Caisleán* Dubh, Maggie sorted through piles of books and various supplies the villagers had donated to help restock the school. Mum helped her divide everything by grade and learning level. Maggie had always believed in allowing students to learn at their own pace, and now she would have the opportunity to establish her own curriculum.

This evening the entire village would descend upon *Caisleán* Dubh for a *céilí*. All the local musicians and singers would perform, everyone would eat, dance and drink, and all who attended would donate money toward the school. Hadn't Riley promised that the more Guinness and Harp that flowed, the looser the purse strings would become? And knowing her brother and Kevin Gilhooley, they would ensure that Mulligan Stew had a full supply.

"A new family moved into Donovan Cottage," Mum said. Mary Donovan had been Fiona Mulligan's best friend since their children started school together decades ago.

"You still miss her." Maggie gave Mum's hand a squeeze. "She'd like knowing her cottage won't sit empty."

Mum sniffled and dabbed the corner of her eye. "Aye, she would at that." She glanced out the window. "I'll take flowers to her, and some to the new family while I'm at it. Wouldn't Mary have done the same?"

"Aye." Maggie drew a deep breath, finishing her sorting. "I think we're almost ready to let Riley deliver the supplies to the school."

Mum nodded and stood beside Maggie to survey the room. "The *céilí* should bring enough to finish the job."

Maggie smiled, unable to suppress the surge of satisfaction that flowed through her. *Pride goeth before a fall.* She shook her head. It didn't matter, because she *was* proud of this, and of her family for thinking of it and helping her make it a reality.

"Would you walk with me to Mary's, lass?"

Maggie hesitated. She had hoped to read some more of the newest book Ailish had sent, but that could wait. Remembering her mother's lingering grief over her old friend's passing, she shoved aside hesitation and flashed the woman a smile. "And what would I rather do than take a walk with you?"

Mum chuckled and rolled her eyes. "If a handsome lad winked your way, you'd change your mind quick enough."

Maggie winced. Mum took every opportunity to drop hints about Maggie's single status. "I've just finished university. There's time."

"There is that." Mum patted Maggie's shoulder. "You've grown into a beautiful woman. Heads will turn tonight."

Maggie gave her mother an indulgent smile. She'd spent most of her life feeling as if she was waiting for something. Or someone. A romantic, silly notion, but there it was.

They gathered flowers outside the cottage. Maggie loved the feel of earth between her fingers and the pungent aroma of growing things. Once they had enough for two nice bouquets, they cut across the field to the road near *Caisleán* Dubh. A chill swept over Maggie as she passed the massive boulders around its foundation.

What's come over you? She couldn't deny that every night she'd slept beneath the newly restored roof of *Caisleán* Dubh, she'd grown more skittish about the place. Perhaps her creepy feelings were a result of having been away so long at school. By the time she'd returned after her first year, her entire family had moved out of Mulligan Cottage and settled in the castle. Even then, she'd longed for the cottage.

She glanced back at the modest cottage where she was raised. More and more, she considered moving back into it. Though she loved her family, a woman her age needed a place of her own.

I'll do it. Later, after they returned from the village, she would discuss the idea with them all. The more she thought about the idea, the better she liked it. After all, the cottage was in good condition and furnished. All she had to do was move her clothes from the castle. The kitchen had everything she would need. She could grow herbs in window boxes, plant more flowers, and make the place really hers. There were cleansing rituals she could utilize . . . just in case.

Just in case of what, Mary Margaret?

She didn't have an answer, and wasn't sure she wanted to hear one anyway. Ailish's ways had been foreign to Maggie, but her curiosity about them was stronger now than while they were rooming together at university. Still, didn't a cleansing feel right somehow? She would do it.

They passed the castle tower and another shiver raced through her. She refused to look at it and tried to concentrate on her mother's chattering.

". . . heard the woman's granddaughter lives with her."

"Whose granddaughter?"

Mum chuckled and shook her head. "And isn't me daughter paying attention to her old mum?"

"Sorry, and you are *not* old." Though Maggie had to admit that Fiona Mulligan was starting to show her age more and more. Her hair had been as red as Maggie's once, but now it was almost completely white. The realization that her mum wasn't immortal didn't set well with Maggie. She supposed it was another part of growing up, but one she didn't have to like.

In silence they followed the bend in the road that hugged the coastline. "What were you saying?" Maggie finally asked, needing to hear the soothing lilt of her mum's voice.

"The woman who moved into Mary's cottage has her granddaughter, so I hear."

"School age?"

"Aileen Gilhooley thought so."

"Well, now, that means we'll have another student."

"So it does."

They stopped first at the cemetery. The ruins of the old church sat at the far end, and the new church—a mere century old now—stood near the road. Overlooking the sea, the cemetery sat on a grassy rise and, as Fiona Mulligan often said, somehow closer to God than most places on this earth.

They lingered at Mary Donovan's grave—the newest in the cemetery. Sensing her mother's need for a bit of privacy, Maggie wandered to Da's grave, where another one waited at his side for his wife.

"If it's all the same to you, Da," she whispered, "I'll be keeping Mum down here with me a good long while yet."

Smiling, Maggie sat beside her da's grave. She had no personal memory of him at all, as she'd still been in nappies when he died. His passing had taken a great toll on the entire family, but they'd survived, just as they had survived her brother Culley's death. In fact, they were stronger for it.

Mum joined Maggie after a bit. "Well, now." The older woman's sigh said much more, and Maggie rose to stand beside her. "Havin' a wee chat with your da, lass?"

"Aye." After several moments of silence, they turned away by unspoken agreement and walked toward Donovan Cottage. It sat on the edge of town nearest the church, the school, and the sea, somewhat isolated from Ballybronagh proper.

"'Tis good to see the new owner is tendin' the flowers," Mum said as Maggie held open the garden gate for her. "A very good thing."

Maggie remembered how much Mary had loved her flowers. Her gardens had kept her going after her husband's death, as her children had all moved away from Ballybronagh.

Mum merely smiled and stepped onto the porch to knock.

A small, white-haired woman opened the door. "Good afternoon," she greeted. "May I help you?"

"I'm Fiona Mulligan, and this is me daughter Maggie," Mum said. "We've come to welcome you to Ballybronagh."

"How nice." The woman smiled, though she glanced nervously beyond them before pushing open the door wide enough for them to enter. "I was just looking to see if my nephew has returned from the market."

"Your nephew, is it?" Mum stepped in ahead of Maggie.

"He ran some errands for us." She smiled apologetically. "I'm afraid we're still settling in, but I have the kettle on, if you've time for a cup."

"Aye. 'Twould be lovely."

Maggie followed the two older women through the familiar house and into the cozy kitchen. All of Mary's furniture was here, bringing back childhood memories. Mum must have been remembering, too.

"Where are my manners?" the woman said, offering her hand to shake Mum's, then Maggie's. "I'm Maureen O'Shea."

"O'Shea, is it?" Mum extended the vase of flowers to their hostess. "'Tis a name we haven't heard in Ballybronagh before."

Pink crept across the woman's cheeks. "No, but my brother-in-law's people came from this area. I think there may be cousins here." She sniffed the blossoms. "Oh, these are just lovely. Thank you. Please call me Maureen."

A beautiful child emerged from a door that led to the upstairs. "Hello," she said, going to her grandmother's side.

Mrs. O'Shea put an arm across her granddaughter's shoulders. The lass stood nearly as tall as her grandmother. "This is my granddaughter, Erin."

After the introductions they all sat at the table and discussed the village, the school, and the *céilí*. Mum made sure the newcomers were invited to the event. "'Twill be a fine chance to meet the villagers."

Mrs. O'Shea smiled. "And we're definitely interested in supporting the school. I purchased this cottage months ago, and had no idea the school was closing."

"But we're savin' it," Mum said. "Maggie here will teach. She went to university to learn how, and she has her diploma to prove it."

Smiling, Maggie remained silent, as did young Erin.

The lass had long blond hair and soft gray eyes. She was nearly the same age as Jacob. They would be Maggie's oldest students, as the older ones would attend secondary school in Kilmurray until they received their leaving papers.

A thrill shot through her. *I'm really going to teach.* Somehow, it was all working out just fine. She would concentrate on the school and work and stop worrying about the castle and the ruins, and the queer feelings she'd had of late.

"You mentioned your brother-in-law's family hailed from here," Mum said. "What would his surname be?"

"Desmond. My nephew is American, though Irish by blood."

"He's my cousin," Erin offered.

"Desmond, you say?" Mum brightened, as Irish were known to do when discussing various lineages. "Aye, there were Desmonds here from way back, though they've all moved across the pond over the years."

"I think the Reardens are related."

"Won't Brady Rearden love hearin' that? He was schoolmaster when me lads were there, givin' him trouble more often than not." Mum gave a satisfied nod. "Isn't that fine, then? And we'll be pleased to welcome young Nick tonight at the *céilí,* too." Mum pushed to her feet. "We'd best be gettin' back to help Bridget."

Maggie rose and shook Erin's hand. "I'll be happy to have you in school, Erin."

"Thank you." The girl smiled shyly.

"And we'll expect you at the *céilí* this evenin'," Mum repeated as they made their way through the house to the front door. "Bring your nephew, too, so we can introduce him to his Cousin Brady."

"Oh, we don't go anywhere without him," Mrs. O'Shea said. She glanced at her granddaughter. "Would you like to go to a party?"

Erin's eyes glittered as she nodded. "Will there be music and dancing?"

Mum laughed. "Joyous music and dancin', lass."

Mrs. O'Shea opened the door and followed them onto the stoop. "We'll be pleased to attend the *céilí*, and so will my nephew."

They bid their farewells and walked along the garden path to the gate. Maggie pushed it open, noticing it still squeaked as it always had.

"It's good to see Mary's things still in the cottage." Mum paused as Maggie secured the gate. "And I think she'd be pleased there is another child in the house."

"Wouldn't she, though?" Maggie caught sight of a tall, dark-haired man carrying a pair of grocery bags across the road. Something about him made her heart press upward against her throat. The way he carried himself? His dark hair? He was too far away to see his face, yet she couldn't stop staring. Couldn't stop wondering.

"Are you all right, Mary Margaret?" Mum asked, shattering the moment.

Maggie nodded, following Mum away from the cottage and the village, toward the tower of *Caisleán* Dubh. Before they reached the bend that would curve toward the sea and Mulligan land, Maggie glanced back over her shoulder at the man who'd stopped at the garden gate to stare after them.

She still couldn't see his face, nor could she stop wondering. Was he Mrs. O'Shea's nephew? Of course, he had to be. She'd said he had gone to market for her, though Maggie had assumed he was much younger.

Maggie kept walking, but couldn't resist the urge to look again before they were too far away. The man still stood there.

Staring.

Three

Nick Desmond had a serious case of lust. It hit him hard and definitely below the belt. The redhead walking away from Aunt Mo's cottage was bright and vibrant and one of the sexiest women he'd ever seen. If that was how they grew them here, Nick would be delighted to get to know the natives a lot better. And he'd thought this job would be boring.

He stood at the gate for several minutes, staring after her, a desperate grip on the grocery bags. His palms itched, and he wished fervently he could touch her. He hadn't seen her *that* closely, but the urge refused to pass.

She had a sweet little wiggle—definitely not the rehearsed kind. Hers was all natural, and so was her hair. He was far from an expert regarding hair color, but he'd be willing to bet hers hadn't come from a bottle.

Knock it off, Desmond. A woman like her wouldn't want a fling with a temporary bodyguard. She'd be looking for something long term. Permanent, even. "Shit."

"Are you coming inside or standing out there all day swearing?" Aunt Mo asked from the stoop.

Startled, Nick shook himself and stepped through the gate. With a squeak that made the hair on the back of his neck stand on end, it slammed behind him. "Remind me to get some WD-40 for that," he said, trying to keep his mind off the redhead.

"She's a pretty one." A knowing smile curved Aunt Mo's lips.

Nick stopped on the walk, staring up at the woman. "Who?"

"My new teacher," Erin said, stepping from the shade of an overgrown shrub. "The lady you were staring at."

Teacher, huh? Nick chuckled, though his cheeks blazed with heat. It was impossible to be cool around these two females. The harder he tried, the worse he failed. "Who, me?"

"Aye, you." Aunt Mo grinned.

"They invited us to a party." Erin all but danced backward as they followed her toward the kitchen. "It's in that big castle called *Caisleán* Dubh."

"Cash-lawn Doov?" Nick echoed.

"Aye. It means Castle Black."

He set the grocery bags on the table, and Aunt Mo started digging through them. "I'm sure you'll have fun at the party," he finally said.

Aunt Mo handed him an apple. "You're going, too."

"Oh. Right."

"Erin, will you run and fetch my purse from my dresser, please?"

"Aye."

The moment the child left the room, Aunt Mo turned on him. "We can't sit in this cottage for the next year, waiting for danger to pass. That's why I hired you."

"Right." He closed his eyes and groaned. "Where you go, I go. Sorry." He didn't bother telling her that he'd been thinking about flings with redheads instead of remembering why he was being paid five grand a week. *Some bodyguard.* "A party in a castle. Got it." *With a gorgeous redhead.*

"And you have a cousin here named Brady Rearden."

"I do?" Nick bit into the apple.

"And you'll meet him tonight." To his amazement, she patted his cheek. "Remember. You're searching for your roots."

He definitely wasn't used to this touchy-feely shit, let alone root searching. "I'm a Desmond, and Desmonds used to live here. Right. Got it. Reardens are my cousins. I just hope there aren't too many of them running around here."

"Only Brady that I know of, and the villagers will want to welcome back one of their own."

"But I'm not—"

"No, but they'll claim you just the same. Family is important here." Aunt Mo smiled again. "I understand how you feel."

Dread settled in his gut. "You do?"

"You haven't socialized much since your father . . ." Her voice trailed away.

"Was murdered," Nick finished, trying not to remember. All the blood. Dad's blood. *My fault.* If only he'd listened . . .

A piece of apple stuck in his throat and he swallowed hard to down it. "Not much socializing." He clenched his teeth and shook his head. He'd used all his spare time trying to prove his father had been murdered, but all he'd accomplished was getting himself framed. Some social life. "And what makes you such an expert?"

She lifted a shoulder and flashed him her sweet little-old-lady smile. "I had you thoroughly investigated, dear." She batted her lashes. "I even know how many times you've been late paying bills."

Nick should have called her a bitch, but, in truth, he was impressed as hell. Besides, good Catholic boys like him didn't call little old ladies—no matter how unusual—bitches. Especially little old ladies who paid their hired help so well. "You amaze me."

"I try hard."

"This is a gravy job. You know that?"

"And I hope it stays that way."

"Yeah, so do I." Nick sobered. "So how many times *was* I late making payments?" He folded his arms, the bitten apple still clutched in his fist.

Her lips twitched. "None."

"Precisely." Nick chuckled, and so did his employer.

Erin bounced into the kitchen with Aunt Mo's purse and looked at them both. "What's so funny?"

"We were just talking about the party," Nick said. "Looks like I'm going, too."

"You'll get to see my pretty teacher again." Erin batted her lashes.

"Ah, she isn't nearly as pretty as you'll be in a few years."

The girl's face pinkened, but he saw the dimple flash in her cheek. "You're just saying that, 'cuz you're my cousin. Right, Mamó?"

"No," Aunt Mo said. "You look like your mum. She had golden hair and gray eyes, too."

"I don't remember her." Erin sighed—something eleven-year-old girls seemed to excel at.

"No, of course you don't." Aunt Mo put the bag of potatoes Nick had bought in the wooden bin beside the back door. "She died when you were just a newborn."

"I don't remember my da either." Erin reached in the bag and found a six-pack of cola. "I've never had this before."

"Never?" Nick reached for a can, definitely willing to change the subject from mobsters to soda. "Every kid oughta have soda. That kinda deprivation is un-American."

Erin giggled. "And wouldn't that be because I'm Irish, silly?"

Nick bit the inside of his cheek and avoided Aunt Mo's gaze. "Whatever. Let's fix this soda deprivation thing right now." He grabbed a glass from the cupboard and looked in the freezer. "No ice?"

Aunt Mo laughed. "The Irish rarely use ice, but I put an old tray in the back there."

"Ah." He broke the ice loose, dropped a few cubes into

a glass, popped the can open, and poured good old Coca-Cola.

Erin stared in awe as he slid the glass toward her and lifted the half-full can. "Cheers," he said, clinking the can against her glass.

"May I, Mamó?" she asked, looking over her shoulder.

"Of course." Aunt Mo looked sad as she watched her granddaughter take her first taste of ordinary soda. "I guess they didn't have this at the abbey school."

"Mmm." Erin licked her foamy moustache. "Oh, isn't this a bit of heaven? We only had juice, water, and milk at school. And the sisters had tea, of course." She burped and covered her mouth, her eyes wide with shame. "Excuse me."

Nick chuckled until he saw the guilt written clearly across Maureen O'Shea's face. The old lady blamed herself for Erin not having a normal childhood.

Their personal lives were none of his business. Still, he barely avoided the urge to pull his employer aside and tell her she'd done the kid a favor by denying her a childhood with a murdering drug lord for a father.

"So what kind of party we going to?" he asked. "Somebody's birthday?"

"No, it's a *céilí*," Erin said, slurping her cola.

"And a *céilí* is . . . ?" He aimed his question at Aunt Mo.

"A celebration with music, dancing, lots of food and . . . beverages."

"Ah, beer." Nick flashed a grin at Erin. "Sounds like a party to me."

"It is a party," Aunt Mo said.

"Oh, beer is bad," Erin said. "The sisters said so."

"Did they now?" Aunt Mo came to Nick's rescue. "And it would be bad if they drank it, or if *you* drank it—at least, before you're of age."

"Didn't those nuns have any sacramental wine?" Nick waggled his eyebrows when the old lady shot him a warn-

ing glare. He took another swig of soda to keep himself
from smarting off again.

"So beer isn't bad?" Erin asked, blinking. "What about
whiskey?"

Nick coughed and set his can aside. "Okay, so we're
going to a *céilí*. Did I pronounce it right?"

Aunt Mo nodded and looked at Erin again. "Alcohol
can be bad if it's abused, Erin," she said very calmly. "Social drinking, as long as you're an adult and not driving
afterward, is different."

"Especially in Ireland." Nick grinned and Aunt Mo
laughed.

"Can I go to the school playground for a while?" Erin
asked.

"*May* I," Aunt Mo corrected.

"May I please go to the school playground for a
while?" Erin repeated. "It's so close you can see it from
here."

Aunt Mo chewed her lower lip and looked at Nick.
"I..."

Time for me to earn my keep. "I'll take her there to
check things out, if it's okay?" His bodyguard job was
part baby-sitting. He'd never imagined himself offering to
go to the playground with a child. Of course, he'd never
been *paid* to do it before either. *Motivation is everything.*

"All right, then." The old woman drew a deep breath
and managed a shaky smile. "It will give you a chance to
see it up close before classes begin."

"Come on, squirt." He headed toward the back door.
"Lock it behind us, and check the front, too," he muttered
as he passed Aunt Mo. "And arm the security system."

She rolled her eyes at him. "I doubt anyone in Ballybronagh locks their doors."

"Maybe not, but you will." He kissed her flushed
cheek, making her eyes widen in surprise. Hey, he was
playing a role and she knew it. "Humor me. I'm a para-
noid American. Besides, what are nephews for?"

"I believe you've kissed the Blarney stone, Nick."

Erin giggled. "Aye, that he has."

Nick paused outside just long enough to hear the lock click from inside. *Stubborn old woman.* But he smiled as he thought it.

The security system had been a problem, and they'd had to select one with an external alarm since there were no monitoring services in this part of Ireland. He needed to talk to the local police about it when he had time.

" 'Tis a fine day." Erin skipped ahead, tossing her blond curls over her shoulder. "Let's race."

Nick ran after her, letting her lead. He had no intention of passing her. He wanted her where he could see her. She was a good kid, and he was glad she didn't look like a Fazzini.

He jogged into the schoolyard behind her and an image flashed through his mind—a man chasing a woman through heavy rain. Where the hell had that come from?

Shaking his head to obliterate the bewildering image, he caught up with a gloating Erin. "You win."

She was winded, but he hadn't even broken a sweat. "But you let me."

He smiled. "Of course."

"Mamó said you were the *garda* back in New York."

"Garda?" Nick tried to remember some of the common Irish words and phrases from the book Aunt Mo had given him. Remembering, a chill swept through him. "Yeah, I was a cop."

"Why'd you quit?" She stood there, staring at him with wide, innocent eyes.

Because your old man wasted my old man, framed me, and turned my career to shit. None of that was the kid's fault, no matter who her father was. Nick squeezed his eyes shut, forcing himself to smile when he reopened them.

"Will you be *garda* here?"

Innocence. He had to remember that. Focus on now and not on the past—at least until his job here was done and he had the evidence he needed to nail Fazzini's ass.

He shrugged. "Who knows?"

"Did I make you sad?" Her brow furrowed. "I ask a lot of questions. Reverend Mother said so."

Nick had to smile. "Hey, I'm not sad because of you, kid." *Because of your old man.*

"Good. I wouldn't like for you to be mad at me."

"Well, now that we've settled all that, let's check out this place."

They both looked across the small cemetery behind the schoolyard. A church sat at one end, complete with a steeple and a brass bell. "This place is like a postcard," he said.

"'Tis beautiful." Erin looked at him again.

For some reason, Nick couldn't stand to look into the child's trusting eyes right now. Most of the time he actually forgot who her father was. Maybe that was for the best.

She tugged on his hand. "Let's go look around the graveyard. Maybe it's *haunted.*"

"Oh, goodie." That earned him another smile, and he figured the discussion about his former career was history now. He breathed a sigh of relief until he heard a board squeak from the schoolhouse steps. He wasn't being much of a bodyguard to let someone sneak up on them from behind.

"Hello again, Erin," a woman said.

They both turned around.

"Oh, look, Nick," Erin said. "My new teacher."

The redhead.

Nick watched her come down the steps toward them. She looked even better up close. All that bright red hair, smooth skin, curves in all the right places. He released a long, slow breath.

"Miss Mulligan," Erin said. "This would be my cousin Nick Desmond, from America."

The teacher smiled. "Hello, Nick Desmond from America."

"You can call him Nick. We do."

Everything about this woman was bright and shiny and pretty. Not beautiful. Pretty. Her laughter sounded like music. Nick couldn't even breathe.

"Welcome to Ballybronagh, Nick Desmond," she said.

"Miss Mulligan." Nick shook the hand she extended. The sudden urge to tug her into his arms and kiss her slammed into him, and he almost staggered from the force of it. *Get a grip.*

"I'd be pleased if you'd call me Maggie."

Her voice was smooth, her skin like cream, her eyes the bluest of blues. "Maggie," he said, holding her hand a beat longer than necessary.

"He thinks you're pretty," Erin said, watching the adult interplay as if storing information for future blackmail. "Mamó said so."

Maggie's rosy blush made the blue of her eyes even bluer. And her mouth. *Man.* Nick wanted to touch his mouth to hers, and . . . *You got it bad, numb-nuts.*

"Well, it's flattered I am." Maggie cleared her throat. "And you're pretty, too."

"Aye, isn't he, though?" Erin giggled.

Maggie laughed again, her bright eyes sparkling. "I meant you, lass, but your cousin here is as well." Her voice fell as she finished her comment.

"Would you want to see inside the school, Erin?"

"Oh, may I?" Erin darted through the open door.

"I think that means yes," he said, smiling at Maggie.

"I suppose it does at that." Maggie took his hand again and gave a little tug. "Come along then, and I'll show you both round."

Nick glanced down at their joined hands and that tightness returned to his chest. *"God. I've missed you,"* Nick thought, looking at her soft mouth again. *"Missed the feel of you in my arms, missed the smell of your hair."*

Where the hell had *that* come from? The ache in his heart had, for a moment, been as profound as . . . as . . . *What?* He shook his head.

Maggie gave him a puzzled look as she paused at the door, staring beyond him. "Did you say something?"

"No." He looked behind him, where she was staring.

"I . . . 'twas nothing, I'm sure." But she looked worried, and kept staring.

"What's over there?" He'd noticed the pile of rubble and what looked like part of a building at the far end of the graveyard.

"The ruins of the old church." She sighed and shook her head. "Did you hear something? 'Tis foolish, I'm being. Enough nonsense. Let's go look at the school."

"Okay." He held the door open, admiring the way her sweater clung to her breasts. He paused on the steps a moment after she'd gone inside.

A prickly sensation eased up the nape of his neck—a feeling he'd experienced often while on the force. Gut instinct. Slowly he looked back toward the ruins and saw something shiny amid the stones.

Fluffy white clouds drifted across the sky, changing the contour of the land from shadowed to sunny every few seconds.

The sun glinted off the shiny object again. Curiosity nudged him to have a closer look. What could be sparkling in that pile of rubble after all this time? Anything of value would have been found by now.

Besides, he had a body to guard inside the school.

And another one to ogle.

Maggie stood at the stove in the newly designed kitchen for *Caisleán* Dubh's Mulligan Stew, stirring one of the sauces Bridget had planned for this evening. This one had beer and sourdough in it. The woman was a marvel. Mum had followed Bridget's recipe, and left Maggie to tend it. The flame was turned low enough not to terrify her, as flames often did.

No one at Mulligan Stew allowed Maggie to cook unsupervised. Her cooking was considered a curse all its own. Oh, she'd improved considerably with Bridget and

Mum to teach her, but she knew her talents did not lie in the realm of pots and pans.

In fact, she didn't really have any unique talents. All she'd ever wanted was to teach, and she prayed she could do it well. She thought of the school again, remembering this afternoon.

Gazing out the arched window that overlooked the coast north of the castle, Maggie recalled Nick Desmond. And wasn't he the handsome one? No man had caught her fancy as quickly and completely before. She didn't even know him, but she couldn't stop thinking about him.

Who was he? What did he do? How long would he stay? Where in America was he from? Absently, she stirred and stirred, while picturing the sight of Nick talking with his young cousin. Coal-black hair and ice-blue eyes fringed with thick lashes a woman would kill for, but they looked perfect right where they were. *Aye, even better.*

And his smile . . . Her heart lurched forward, dancing a wee jig as she remembered his smile. Quick and a little guarded, perhaps, but definitely a smile to melt a woman's heart. The man had a wicked charm about him, though she sensed some reserve as well. Nick Desmond was a man with secrets.

"By the saints, save us all," Riley muttered from the doorway.

"I'm only stirring it," Maggie said, rolling her eyes. "Mum prepared it from Bridget's recipe. I've added absolutely nothing, so stop your blathering."

"Thank the Blessed Virgin." Riley crossed himself.

Maggie stuck her tongue out at him.

"Jaysus, Mary, and Joseph, but some things never change," Mum muttered through a grin as she entered the kitchen carrying two pies. "These are cool now. With the food the others will bring, we'll have more than enough."

"And Kevin is setting up his wares near the archway," Riley said. "I'm sure he's needing a hand or two about now."

"Aye, and the Guinness will need to be sampled, of course." Maggie grinned at her brother.

"'Tis my duty as an Irishman." He straightened with pride.

"Then get on with you, lad," Mum said, shooing him away. "Bridget will be down in a few minutes, and we have everything under control."

Riley kissed Mum's cheek. "Thank you for making her go for a kip. She needs more rest just now."

"She's doing fine, lad. Don't worry yourself so." Mum waved him out of the kitchen again and glanced in the pot Maggie still stirred. "Smells like nectar fit for angels."

Maggie sniffed appreciatively. "Aye, it does at that. Bridget said she'll be adding cheese to it later."

"Swiss. You'll want to get prettied up for this evening," she added quietly.

Maggie slid her mother a glance, wondering if she'd read her thoughts about Nick Desmond. No, of course not, but Maggie *did* find herself wanting to look her best this evening. She usually didn't bother with anything more than clean and presentable, but . . . well . . .

Listen to yourself.

"Thanks for understanding about me moving into the cottage," Maggie said, still amazed that no one but Riley had objected. Of course, Bridget had handled him with ease. The memory still made Maggie smile. "I just feel . . . a need for my own space, I guess."

Mum appeared thoughtful. "'Tis a sign that you're ready to settle down." Her lips twitched, and she added, "Like a bird building its nest."

"I am *not* building a nest." Maggie's cheeks flamed at the implication.

"Of course not. I'm understandin' the need for your own place just fine, lass, but the smudgin' business is another matter entirely."

Maggie lifted a shoulder and smiled. "It's a . . . cleansing. At least that's what Ailish said. I bought a book about feng shui, too."

"Whatever." Fiona Mulligan smiled in her tolerant way. "Aileen called. She said Maureen O'Shea's nephew, Nick Desmond, is a man full grown, and is kind on the eyes as well. What are you going to wear, lass?"

And didn't you change the subject quick enough, Fiona Mulligan? Maggie almost laughed aloud at her mother's skill. "I'll wear the blue dress you made me for graduation," she said, deciding not to react to her mother's hinting. After all, she'd already seen Nick Desmond with her own eyes, and definitely agreed with Aileen's assessment. *Oh, aye.*

"That dress is lovely on you—Mulligan blue, like your eyes." Mum smiled and took the long-handled spoon from Maggie. "I'll finish this, lass. You go change for the *céilí*."

Maggie kissed her mother's cheek. "Thanks. I'll do that."

The cottage was just across the meadow from the castle. Soon, she was staring at herself in the bathroom mirror, wondering why she ever bothered trying to wear make-up. "You've got it all arseways."

First she didn't have enough. Then she had too much. She washed it off three times before she gave up and settled for a bit of powder and lipstick. She was who she was, and no fancy paint would change that. She left her wild red curls down, adding a glittery comb Jacob had given her last Christmas to hold her bangs.

Wearing the blue silk dress that left her shoulders bare, she walked back across the meadow to the castle. The weather was mild for August, but it wouldn't last. However, this evening was fine and amazingly clear. Fog would roll in by morn', of course.

A shiver skittered through her, and she hugged herself against a sudden chill, like the one she felt each time the voices came to her. She'd almost made out words at the schoolhouse today. So she'd thought.

The knowledge that Riley had heard *Caisleán* Dubh's whispering after their brother Culley's death forced her to accept the existence of things no one could readily explain. And Bridget had heard it, too. Surely the voices Maggie now heard weren't a sign that the curse had returned?

She crossed herself and drew a shaky breath, reminding herself that Riley and Bridget's love had broken the curse. All was well now. *Caisleán* Dubh was a place of joy—not evil.

"Aye, and don't you be forgetting it." She forced the disturbing thoughts to the back of her mind. For now.

A steady flow of guests walked from the village toward *Caisleán* Dubh, carrying bowls, pans, and musical instruments. Séamus Doone even had his pipes. The castle would be livelier than a Saturday night at Gilhooley's Pub.

Hope soared through Maggie. They *would* raise enough money to keep the Ballybronagh School open this year. And, perhaps, the next . . . ?

A smile curved her lips just as she spotted the tallest man in the crowd. At dusk his hair appeared even darker, but he was unmistakable even without good light. Nick Desmond. A shiver raced through Maggie that had nothing to do with the temperature.

"There's Miss Mulligan," young Erin called. "Oh, and isn't that the prettiest dress?"

Maggie fell in step beside them. "Thank you, Erin." She noticed the child's fancy party dress, which must have cost a dear amount. "Yours is pretty, too."

"Thank you. Mamó bought it for my birthday."

"Erin just turned eleven last month," Mrs. O'Shea offered.

Maggie complimented the woman's cream-colored silk and pearls. With her white hair, it gave her an almost angelic appearance. Again she couldn't help but notice the quality of her clothing. Maureen O'Shea was obviously a woman of means. How odd that she'd chosen to settle in modest little Donovan Cottage, not to mention Ballybronagh itself. But it was none of Maggie's business.

Nick remained silent, walking on Erin's far side. He wore jeans and a dark shirt. Unfortunately, the waning twilight kept her from seeing the colors, but inside the castle she would again see both that *and* his beautiful eyes. Warmth blazed in her cheeks at the prospect. She hadn't felt this way since her first date. *'Tis foolish you're acting, Maggie.* She was the local teacher, and she should behave in a mature and respectable manner.

Then why did her hands perspire with the thought of seeing her student's handsome cousin again? Why did her tummy quiver and her insides turn warm and fluid? *Now, aren't you going all silly-soft?*

They followed the line of people through the massive front doors of *Caisleán* Dubh. It never failed to shock her each time she entered this way, after all the years of having the castle sealed. The renovations were complete on the main level and in the family's living quarters, but the tower was still off-limits until the workers completed the restoration. That section of the castle would be for overnight guests.

Maggie had planned to break away from the merry crowd and enter through the kitchen door the family typically used. But, somehow, she found herself wanting to remain right here with all the others.

Of course, she really only wanted to stay close to one person. Even as she rolled her eyes at her own foolishness, she found herself beside the cause of her nonsensical behavior. His warmth radiated through his sleeve and into her.

So much sex appeal in one body should be illegal. Why, he fairly made her swoon just walking at her side. How, in heaven's name, would she react if he ever . . . ever . . .

Get on with you, Mary Margaret.

She felt like a bloody fool. Gathering the remnants of her dignity about her, she looked up at him as the lights of the main hall bathed him in a golden glow. He looked like a movie star, all spiffed up and handsome enough to make a lass fall at his feet. Oh, and wouldn't that make her feel mature and dignified?

"Jaysus, Mary, and Joseph," she muttered, swallowing the sudden lump in her throat.

"I'm sorry," he said, leaning down. "Did you say something?"

Maggie gave a nervous laugh. "Nothing important." *Me acting like an eejit, is all.*

"I'm going to take this cake to the tables over there," Mrs. O'Shea said. "Erin, you come with me. Nick, why don't you get us all something cool to drink? Maybe they have an orange squash or lemonade for Erin?"

"I want more of that soda Nick bought at the market," Erin said.

Nick chuckled and said, "Only if your grandma says it's okay, squirt. It has caffeine in it."

"Hmm." Mrs. O'Shea looked down at Erin, then up at Nick. "Too much caffeine will stunt your growth. You may have one cola, Erin, then switch to something without caffeine." The older woman's eyes twinkled. "Someone should've given your cousin more of it while he was a child, so he wouldn't be so tall."

Erin giggled and Nick rolled his eyes. Maggie thought he looked absolutely delicious. The thought shocked her, but the notion stuck. *Aye, delicious.*

"You might like Cidona," she heard herself say.

"What would that be?" Erin asked.

"Fizzy apple cider."

"Oh, I do like the fizzies."

"We'll go see about all these fine cakes and pies now," Mrs. O'Shea said. "My sweet tooth is feeling a wee bit deprived."

"Don't you want me to hang close to you and Erin?" Nick raised his eyebrows as he met his aunt's gaze.

The woman appeared thoughtful, but finally shook her head. "Only villagers are here. We'll be fine. I haven't attended a *céilí* since . . . Oh, not since I was a lass." She patted her nephew's flushed cheek. "Maybe Maggie will introduce you to some more young people."

Nick narrowed his gaze as he watched Maureen weave through the crowd with Erin in tow. Fiona Mulligan intercepted them and started introducing them about.

"They'll be fine," Maggie said. "Mum will take good care of them." Wasn't it sweet, the way he worried after his aunt and cousin?

"Yeah, I suppose." He looked around the great hall, almost as if memorizing the place. "I'd feel better if there weren't so many people here."

"It's a fund-raiser for the school," Maggie reminded him. "More people means more money raised."

"True." He flashed her a cockeyed grin that stole her breath. "And that's a knockout dress."

Flustered by the sudden compliment, Maggie blinked and smiled. "Well, now, isn't that a nice thing to say? Thank you." She took in his midnight-blue shirt and black jeans. "You look fine, too." *Much better than fine.*

"Let's check out the bar." Nick crooked an arm toward her and Maggie found herself looping hers through it.

Oh, my. He was all hardness and heat and . . . and *man.* Now *that* was mature. She obviously needed lessons in public behavior around gorgeous men. It wasn't as if she'd never dated at university. Oh, and what a fascinating curriculum such lessons would entail.

"What's your pleasure?" Nick asked.

"Harp, please," she said.

"A glass, Maggie?" Kevin Gilhooley asked, sliding curious looks at Nick.

"Please." She smiled when Riley loomed beside Kevin, arching his eyebrows questioningly toward her companion. "Riley, this is Nick Desmond, cousin to Brady. Nick, this is my brother, Riley Mulligan."

"Pleased to meet you," Riley returned, thrusting out his hand. *"Céide Mílé Fáilte."*

"Uh . . . is that good or bad?"

Maggie laughed again. "It means a hundred thousand welcomes, so that would be good."

"Thanks."

The two giants shook hands as Maggie looked from one to the other, amazed to realize they were almost the same height. Was it her imagination, or were they having a bloody contest to see which one could squeeze the other's hand the hardest? *Men!*

"You'll do," Riley said, grinning as he released Nick's hand.

"Do for what?" Nick asked, flexing his fingers.

"Arm wrestling." Riley slapped the bar with the flat of his palm. "We'll be having a contest at Gilhooley's next Saturday night—strictly to raise money for the school." He winked at Maggie.

"If I can get away, I'll be happy to donate the bones in my hand to the cause." That delightful crooked grin spread across Nick's face again.

Riley threw his head back and laughed. Kevin slid a pint of Guinness onto the tray holding drinks for Maureen and Erin O'Shea. "'Tis on the house, boyo," he said in his best publican voice. "To ease the *pain.*"

"It's getting deep in here." Nick chuckled and shook his head. "Didn't bring a shovel."

"Aye, and it'll get a lot deeper from the look of the flow of liquid refreshments," Maggie said indulgently. "But 'tis for a good cause." She patted her brother on the hand. "I'll help Nick deliver these drinks."

Maggie couldn't help noticing how tense Nick seemed as he scanned the throng for his aunt and cousin. He suddenly relaxed, and she realized he must have spotted them at the same time Maggie had. Mum was teaching the children a folk dance while Séamus Doone played his pipes, and Sean Collins joined with a traditional *bodhrán.* Mrs. O'Shea clapped her hands in delight, her eyes dancing as happily as the children.

As they finished the number, Brady Rearden went to her side and bowed, kissing her hand.

"Your cousin Brady's a charmer," Maggie said, laughing. "And doesn't it appear he's flirting with your aunt?"

"He's my mysterious cousin? Well, I'll be." Nick shook his head, though he still wore that potent smile of his.

Mum's eyes twinkled as she took the tray of beverages from Nick. "You all go dance while I take Erin and Jacob to fill their plates." Then, of course, she turned her attention to Maggie and Nick. "And introduce young Nick to his cousin Brady. 'Tis so sweet to find long, lost cousins."

Maggie gave her mother a kiss on the cheek.

"Go on with you now." Fiona Mulligan scrubbed away her tears. "I'll enjoy seeing Brady's expression when he meets his own cousin."

Brady approached them and took Nick's hand. "So you're the Desmond, then?"

"I'm Nick Desmond."

"And your da's given name, lad?" Brady listened intently, his keen eyes studying Nick as he waited.

Nick tensed. "John."

"Aye, son of Liam." Brady embraced Nick, obviously startling the man. "Welcome home, lad. Welcome home."

"Uh, thanks."

After much back pounding, Fiona nudged them all toward the dance floor again. She had the children busy filling their plates. "Off with you now. The music's startin'."

Mum had no shame, and Maggie knew better than to argue. Unfortunately, Mum knew that, too.

"Well, then." Maggie surrendered her beer and turned to face the most delicious-looking man she'd ever been forced to dance with. *Aye, and isn't it a hardship?*

Nick watched Mrs. O'Shea and Brady swing onto the dance floor like a couple half their age. Shaking himself, he looked at Maggie. "What did you say? Sorry."

"We'll have to dance, Nick," she said. "Either that or explain why not to my Mum, and I'm not that brave. Are you?"

Nick gripped her shoulder and turned her to face him. When she did, he gently clasped her upper arms. Maggie's breath froze. His touch was warm and gentle—his eyes dark and mesmerizing.

"You'll have to teach me the steps." He lifted a shoulder and released a sigh that eased through her.

She took him by the hand and led him into the crowd. Warmth stole through her as she met Bridget's knowing smile from where she stood near the entrance to the kitchen.

Maggie couldn't stop herself from wanting to touch Nick any more than she could prevent her next breath. A strange ache in her heart made her yearn for this man, and her body was none too shy about it either.

Maybe he had secrets. Maybe not. All she knew was that she wanted to know him better. Much better. She stopped to face him, feeling suddenly shameless and daring. Maybe even a little sexy.

Nick's teeth flashed as he smiled again.

She did love his smile.

"Where in America are you from, Nick?" she asked, needing to break the spell that had woven itself around them.

"New York." He lifted a shoulder. "Born and raised. I guess that's no secret."

Aye, but something is. Why was she so certain of that? More importantly, why did she want to spend time with him despite that certainty?

He held her hand in both of his now, sweeping his thumbs in circles across her knuckles. "There's something about you. I just had an overwhelming urge to . . . to . . ."

Aye, and didn't she understand what he meant by urges just now? It took Maggie a few heartbeats to recover from the shock of awareness that rippled through her at his touch. "Dance?" she finally whispered. Why couldn't she put two intelligent words together around this man?

"Right. Dance." He gazed toward the tall windows, open to the evening air.

An almost-full moon cast a silver streak across the water. "'Tis beautiful," she said, drawing a shaky breath as the music surrounded them, wrapping them in a cocoon of intimacy.

"Beautiful." He dropped his hands to her waist. "You're going to think I'm crazy, and I'm not so sure you'd be wrong."

Maggie bit her lower lip, baffled by the powerful pull she felt toward this man. "Tell me."

"There's something about you. It's like . . . I know you, but I don't."

Her breath caught in her throat. Blood pulsed hotly through her veins, as if a potent drug had overtaken her senses.

He took a step closer, lowering his face toward hers. His breath was warm against her, and the thrumming of her pulse grew stronger, louder, more demanding. A deep longing eased through her.

"Not now. Not here," she whispered, sensing he wanted to kiss her. And didn't she want that more than anything?

"Not here," he agreed, his expression intense. "Soon."

She nodded, for she could do nothing more as they began to dance. Aye. He would kiss her.

There was no force on earth powerful enough to stop this. To stop him.

To stop them.

Four

At the first hint of dawn Nick woke up in his room off the kitchen of what everyone called Donovan Cottage, even though no one named Donovan lived there now. Watery sunlight leaked in around the frilly curtains as he rubbed his eyes and climbed out of bed. He staggered naked to the window to gaze out at the ground-hugging mist.

Memories of last night's party haunted him. He hadn't attended a large social gathering since Dad's death. Despite his initial concerns for Aunt Mo and Erin's safety in such a large crowd, he'd actually relaxed and enjoyed himself.

He rolled his eyes. Relaxed wasn't exactly the right word—especially not with regard to Maggie Mulligan. He released a long sigh. Who was she, and why couldn't he stop thinking about her? He'd dreamed about kissing her all night. Only kissing. For now. Of course, other parts of his anatomy had something more intimate in mind. And dreams of Maggie Mulligan were much, much better than his usual nightmares.

Don't go there. He quelled the images by remembering Maggie—her sweetness, her brightness, her beauty.

The woman turned him on—no denying that. His morning erection throbbed, reminding him just how long it had been since he'd been laid. Still, what had Dad said? *Don't let the little head do the thinking for the big head.*

Even as Nick acknowledged the thought, guilt swam through him. Maggie wasn't the kind of woman a guy could have a casual affair with and walk away.

And Nick Desmond—the crippled shell he was now—wasn't the kind of guy who could offer a woman anything more.

Even so, he would see her again, and the thought pleased him. He glanced pointedly down at his blatant erection. He'd just have to keep that in his pants. But remembering how she'd felt in his arms, and how desperately he wanted to kiss her, that would be far easier said than done.

He turned his attention back to the scenery. It had rained some during the night, but this morning there were breaks in the clouds where sunlight painted pink streaks across the sky. His gaze drifted across the treeless landscape separating the cottage from the sea. To his left the dark tower of *Caisleán* Dubh dominated everything for as far as he could see. To his right the schoolhouse and church sat perched above the sleepy village.

"It's like frigging Brigadoon, only Irish," he muttered. As he stared at the ruins of the original church, the sharp rays of the rising sun broke through the clouds and bathed the area with light.

Something glittered from the pile of stones, and Nick gripped the windowsill. He shook his head and forced himself away from the window. It was probably nothing more than a gum wrapper. Right?

"Don't be an ass."

That place called to him and gave him the creeps at the same time. A good run would put his imagination *and* his libido to rest for a while. Aunt Mo and Erin never rose before eight, so he could easily return before they stirred.

His employer had arranged for a security system and had all the locks changed before their arrival, thank God.

After pulling on sweats and running shoes, he made sure the doors were locked and did some stretches before heading out toward the sea. He picked up speed as he ran away from the village, toward the road that curved past the school and church.

Blood pounded through his veins; sweat trickled down his face, neck, and into his sweatshirt. The ground was somewhat spongy, giving him an even better workout. He needed to run every day. It kept him sane.

While on the force he'd gone to the gym every day to keep in shape. One more thing he missed about his job— the department gym. With the money piling up in his bank account back home now, he'd be able to buy his own damned gym.

After he put Fazzini behind bars.

As always, the mere thought of that name sent savage rage kicking through Nick. He clenched his teeth, his fists pumping at his sides as his legs stretched toward the sea. Fazzini would pay for his father's murder.

"Burn, witch, burn."

Nick stumbled and fell, skidding along the wet grass. *"Burn, witch, burn."* There it was again.

His breathing ragged, Nick pushed himself to his knees and mopped sweat from his brow. Wet grass stains and mud smeared the elbows and knees of his sweats. Slowly he pushed to his feet, dragging his trembling fingers through his damp hair.

Fazzini was more devil than witch. Why had those words echoed through Nick's mind? More importantly, who had said them?

He swallowed hard and heard the distant sound of ringing bells. He turned slightly to gaze at the church, but its bell was stationary and silent. Besides, the sound Nick heard was too faint to have come from nearby.

For that matter, how had he ended up back here? He'd meant to run toward the sea and beyond the castle, then circle back toward Ballybronagh. He must have turned this way without paying attention.

Brushing off some of the loose grass and mud, he wandered beyond the church and across the schoolyard. The sun drifted behind a cloud, then reappeared a moment later to shine on the old ruins. Again something shiny winked at him from the debris.

Nick Desmond was going to chase down a gum wrapper—or whatever it was—and put his imagination to rest once and for all. He glanced at his watch. With over an hour left before Aunt Mo and Erin would rise, he might as well satisfy his curiosity.

He meandered through the cemetery and leapt over the low stone wall. The moment his feet touched ground on the opposite side, an eerie feeling washed over him, similar to what he'd felt at a murder scene early in his career. The senior officer had told him the place was haunted.

Nick looked over his shoulder and shook himself. "Enough of this crap."

He stepped over crumbling, moss-covered stones and could clearly make out the foundation of the original church. The place hadn't been very large—probably about half the size of the newer one.

He nudged a stone aside and watched dozens of earthworms squiggle in protest. The scents of mud and mold filled his nostrils. Ireland had more than its share of both.

Again the sun played hide and seek. He stood, waiting. Hoping.

"I lost it once, and I shall not lose it again, if only I can find it."

"Whoa . . ." Nick bit his lower lip, wondering why strange words and voices popped into his head around here. The same thing had happened yesterday when he'd first met Maggie in the schoolyard.

The voice present in his head—*now that sounds sane*—was different than the one about the witch. "You are losing it, Desmond."

He shook his head, determined to put it all out of his

mind with a hot shower before Aunt Mo and Erin started wondering where he was. So why the hell didn't he turn around and haul his ass back to the cottage now?

Something held him here. Bizarre but true. He swallowed hard, drew in a shaky breath, and waited. . . .

A flash of brilliant sunlight shone down through the clouds again, pointing toward a shiny object. Of course, the mere notion of the sun deliberately pointing at anything sounded nuts, but Nick couldn't shake the certainty. He rushed toward a large, mossy stone near what appeared to have been a fireplace once upon a time.

Something silver hid amid centuries worth of mud and moss. He trembled with a curious sense of urgency as he scraped the area clean with his fingernails and pried loose what appeared to be a piece of jewelry. It had practically become part of the stone itself after all this time, and nature was reluctant to release the treasure to a mere human.

"I've found it!"

Nick looked around as he rose with the mud-encrusted metal cradled in his palm. After nudging away more filth, he realized it was a badly tarnished, silver crucifix. Again that eerie feeling crept over him, and his breath snagged in his throat.

"I've searched so long. . . ."

Nick wanted to explore more, but a desperate need to clean the crucifix and hide it away drove him back to the cottage. He removed his mud-caked shoes on the back stoop and punched in the code to disarm the security system.

Safe in his room, he examined the intricately molded silver again. He had no idea of its age, but it could be worth a bundle. Transferring the heavy metal from palm to palm, he watched the play of light across the crucified figure of Jesus, his heart racing. He cradled it beneath the sunlight, his eyes stinging.

"Jeez, Desmond," he said to himself as he scrubbed his eyes.

"Nick?" A gentle knock sounded on his door.

Aunt Mo. He had to hide his treasure. Guilt kicked him in the gut, but he shoved the crucifix into a drawer full of socks, then opened his bedroom door.

"Yeah?" His voice sounded gruff, clogged by the freaky emotions churning through him.

"Well, top o' the mornin' to you, too," Aunt Mo said, a curious expression on her face. Her gaze drifted down the length of him. "Been out playing in the mud already, have you?"

He forced a chuckle and leaned casually against the doorjamb. "Sorry for being so grouchy. Need a shower and caffeine."

"Aye, so I see." She patted his arm. "I'll put the kettle on, lad."

Nick sighed. "Tea again?"

"Oh, I think I can find a bit of coffee to sweeten you up." Aunt Mo's laughter followed her as she turned toward the kitchen. Nick closed the door and retrieved the crucifix again, wondering why it affected him so. It wasn't as if he'd been to mass recently. In fact, the last time he'd set foot in church had been for Dad's memorial service.

Unnerved, Nick released a long, slow breath, trying to think of logical, practical reasons for keeping his find a secret. Carefully, he tucked it into a sock in the bottom of his drawer, vowing to find some silver polish and give it a good going over later.

In the shower it came to him. He had to keep the crucifix to himself to protect his employer and Erin. It made perfect sense, really. It was his duty. If the item proved to have any monetary or historical value, Ballybronagh could find itself filled with treasure-seeking strangers. Even media. That could be dangerous if anyone recognized the allegedly dead Maureen Fazzini.

As he dressed and wrapped the silver cross in a tissue before tucking it into his pocket, he knew he was lying to himself. His real reason for not sharing his discovery with anyone was that he feared the authorities might confiscate it, claiming it belonged to the village or county. For some inexplicable reason, he couldn't bear to part with it yet. Maybe not ever.

"Mine."

Maggie opened her eyes to sunshine and smiled. Dreams of Nick Desmond had left her feeling oddly happy. Granted, the man was good-looking enough that he should be illegal, but that wasn't enough to explain her powerful attraction to him.

She sat up and swung her legs over the side of the bed, marveling that this cottage was now hers. Built over a century ago, it was sturdy and well kept. Maggie simply loved it. She never wanted to live anywhere else.

Thoughtful, she meandered downstairs and wandered through the place. Her home. After sealing *Caisleán* Dubh to protect the family from that wretched curse, this house had become the Mulligans' sanctuary. Generations of tragedies had suddenly ceased, with the exception of Maggie's father, Patrick, who had entered the castle on the day of his death. No one ever discovered what had driven the man to enter the forbidden structure, but enter he had—a decision which cost him his life.

Maggie wished she could have known her da. Still, she liked to believe that her strong, honorable brothers were much like Da must have been. If only Culley . . .

Sighing, she went to the kitchen and waited for the kettle to boil, then wet the tea leaves. Dear Culley had traveled to America on holiday after graduating from university. There, he had met Bridget and fallen in love. A few days after their elopement, he died in a car accident. Though they'd lost Culley, they now had Bridget and their son Jacob. And wasn't it a miracle that Bridget had come to Ireland and fallen in love with yet another Mulligan after all these years? That miracle had broken the curse on *Caisleán* Dubh at long last.

She glanced up at the west window, where the castle's dark tower thrust upward. Fingers of ice left prints along her spine. "Being foolish this morning, are you, Maggie?" Still, she couldn't prevent the odd sense of foreboding from gripping her each time she gazed upon the tower.

Slowly she turned away from the window and surveyed the kitchen—her kitchen. She loved this cottage and the memories it held. Now it was hers. Legally, of course, it was part of the Mulligan estate, but wasn't she a Mulligan and proud of it? Besides, she never wanted to live anywhere but here in Ballybronagh, near her family.

"And isn't the cottage near enough?" She smiled to herself.

Oh, she loved her family as much or more than most women her age. Even so, this bit of privacy suited her. Here, she could come and go as she pleased, invite friends over for dinner—as long as she didn't poison them with her bad cooking, of course—and, perhaps, even have a wild, romantic affair.

Heat settled low in her belly as an image of Nick flashed through her mind. A smile curved her lips as she poured tea into her cup, then sat at the old, scarred table with her calendar and her memories.

She'd never had an affair. Savoring a sip of warm, bracing tea, she closed her eyes and remembered how it had felt to dance with Nick, to watch his eyes darken as he gazed at her. At *her*—Maggie Mulligan.

She wasn't very experienced where men were concerned, but Bridget had told her that a woman could sense these things. Bridget and Riley had wanted each other before they'd fallen in love. Love and lust went well together, but Maggie could see now that sometimes lust worked alone, and it was certainly too early to think about love.

Lust, however, was another matter entirely. Aye, she lusted after Nick Desmond. Her cheeks warmed and she gave a nervous laugh. Wouldn't Mum swoon if she could have read her daughter's thoughts about now? Still, Maggie was old enough to know about sex and the wanting of it, even if she hadn't actually *experienced* it.

Ah, but Nick . . . She closed her eyes, remembering the warmth of his strong hands on her shoulders, the heat of longing pumping through her veins, the powerful urge to pull him against her and kiss him. And more . . .

"Whew!" She fanned herself and rolled her eyes, forcing herself to focus on the calendar spread out before her. Brady had agreed to go over the school schedule with her today, and she wanted a rough one sketched out before then.

After scribbling a few notes, she ate a quick breakfast and set off toward town. As she passed the castle, guilt nudged her. She should stop in and greet her family, but for some reason she couldn't make her feet go in that direction. Besides, she had an appointment with Brady at the school, and she didn't want to keep him waiting.

Biting her lower lip, she vowed to stop in on her way back and drew a deep breath, her gaze riveted to the school and church at the edge of town. In only a few weeks school would be in session, and she would be working at her first real job. Though her salary was minimal, it was more than enough. She had the cottage and shared in the crops and wholesale food items ordered for Mulligan Stew.

Aye, everything was working out beautifully. She had her own home, enough privacy, and was about to fulfill her lifelong dream of teaching at this very school.

So why did she feel so restless? *'Tis your imagination again, Maggie.* No, more than that. She had a yearning for something—almost as if she'd lost it and had to find it again. Of course, that was a silly notion, and one she'd best forget. She had enough work to do without dwelling on stuff and nonsense.

As she passed the church a young woman came running down the steps toward her. "Maggie, is that you?" the young woman asked. "I saw all that red hair from clear across the field. It *is* you."

"Aye, but . . ." She looked at the woman's short-cropped blonde curls and wide green eyes. Recognition teased her memory, and she had a sudden flash of those same eyes beneath the brim of her brother's cap when she'd tried to sneak her way onto the lads-only soccer team. "Irene Gilhooley, as I live and breathe!"

They hugged and chattered about childhood memories. Finally, Maggie asked, "Are you back for good then?"

"We'll see." Irene smiled, a dimple flashing in her cheek. "Aren't I part owner of Gilhooley's, after all?"

"Truly? You mean that ornery Kevin decided to let a mere lass join the business?"

Irene grinned again. "Da didn't give him any choice in the matter. I always have been half owner, but was too young and too busy seeing the world with Mum and Da to do anything about it."

Irene's parents had won the Irish Lottery during her sixth year of school. They'd immediately packed up their youngest child and moved to Crete. Maggie didn't remember seeing her since. Kevin, being much older, had stayed to take over his parents' pub. "So now you're back to help your aunt keep your brother in line?"

Irene laughed. "And to find myself. Let's get together over a bottle of wine and I'll tell you all about it."

"I'd like that." Maggie immediately recognized one of the things that had been missing in her life since returning to Ballybronagh. Friends. Most of the lasses she'd grown up with, including her best friend, had moved to Dublin, since jobs in small villages like Ballybronagh were hard to come by. Only a few were still in the area, and they were all married with children. In fact, some of their youngest ones would be Maggie's students. Her college roommate, Ailish, was her only truly close friend, and she missed her.

"Where are you off to now?"

Irene's words brought Maggie back to the present. "School. I'm the new teacher." Pride made her smile as she glanced at her watch. "And I'm late for a meeting. I'll come by Gilhooley's after."

Irene gave her another quick hug. "I'll be there, showing Kevin how to organize things better. 'Tis driving him off his nut, I am."

Irene's laughter as she walked away told Maggie that the woman enjoyed tormenting poor Kevin more than anything. Remembering all the times she and her brothers had bickered and teased each other made her smile and shake her head. As Mum often said, *some things never change.* Like Maggie's bad cooking . . .

Chuckling at herself, she walked across the schoolyard and climbed the steps to the back stoop. A soft breeze blew in from the sea, carrying with it the sound of voices raised in anger, almost in a sort of chant. She couldn't quite make out the words, but she couldn't deny the sudden panic that made her belly clench and her throat tighten. Even without looking, she knew there were no people arguing nearby, no one between her and the sea.

No one alive.

And isn't that the craziest notion?

Any crazier than cursed castles and reincarnation? Didn't she believe that Riley and Bridget had heard *Caisleán* Dubh's whispering? Aye, especially after they broke the curse.

She swallowed hard and glanced over her shoulder, toward the ruins. Odd that the voices she heard had nothing at all to do with *Caisleán* Dubh. A shiver skittered down her spine.

Or did they?

Five

Angelo Fazzini junior stood in his mother's suite of rooms in the east wing of their Long Island home. He was all alone now. No wife, no children, no parents. No one to carry on the Fazzini name or empire. He needed an heir. Maybe he should remarry.

Of course, that wouldn't bring Mother back. Still devastated from the shock of her sudden death, he walked around her sitting room, touching things that had belonged to her. A curio cabinet filled with figurines from Ireland stood untouched against the far wall.

His breath snagged in his throat and he squeezed his eyes shut for a few seconds, reeling in his emotions. He couldn't afford to spend weeks in mourning. He had pending business on hold already. He would finish his mourning today, then get back to work.

The news of his mother's private plane crashing into the Atlantic had devastated him. She had always been so strong, so proud, so disapproving. He smiled sadly, remembering the last time she'd tried to convince him to give up the business his father had worked so hard to create. Of course, Angelo couldn't do that. He'd promised his father that he would make them bigger and stronger

than ever. And he had. Mother simply hadn't understood
business. Of course, Angelo had also promised not to tell
his half brother they had the same father. That still tore at
him.

He crossed the room and opened the door of the walnut
curio cabinet, removing the small figure of a faerie resting
on a shamrock. Mother had enjoyed these whimsical
things. Worthless things. Still, he smiled, remembering.

From there, he glanced toward her small antique desk
near the bay window. A light flashing on the phone drew
his attention, and he crossed the room still clutching the
figurine.

There was a message on her machine. An overwhelming need to hear her voice on the outgoing message
gripped him, so he pushed that button first. Holding his
breath, he waited.

He heard his mother's soft, lilting voice as she asked
the caller to leave a message after the tone. *How can she
be dead?*

Then he pushed the PLAY button to hear the new message left on her machine. As the electronic beep sounded,
he reached for the STOP button, but a small voice made
him freeze.

"Mamó, when are you coming for—"
Scowling, Angelo hit rewind and listened to the voice
again. A child. Why would a child have called his mother?

Mamó. "Where have I heard that before?" He played
the message again and again, struggling with memories
better left buried—his disastrous marriage, their beautiful
baby girl, her kidnapping and murder.

Why did the sound of some kid's voice on an answer-
ing machine make him remember that nightmare? The
call was probably nothing more than a wrong number.
Even so, he listened again, a cold sweat coating his fore-
head and his palms. His gut clenched and his throat tight-
ened. It wasn't the child's voice that had triggered those
memories.

Mamó. That one word. He looked at his mother's